THE DUCK STREET GANG

The headmaster's announcement that the nativity play will be done by Class 2D dismays the teachers at Duck Street School. Class 2D themselves are the only ones looking forward to it. Nellie Allbright, Johnno, Brain and the rest have their own ideas about nativity plays. Their 'original' interpretation is a triumph – and a riot!

This is just one of the hilarious stories of escapades, adventures and mishaps starring The Duck Street Gang.

Dedicated to:

Mrs McCobb, who did all my typing,
and to my niece Denise Hirrel,
who did nothing but insists on being mentioned.

The Duck Street Gang

DENIS MARRAY

A Magnet Book

First published in Great Britain 1984
by Hamish Hamilton Children's Books
This Magnet edition published 1986
by Methuen Children's Books
11 New Fetter Lane, London EC4P 4EE
Reprinted 1987
Copyright © 1984 Denis Marray
Printed in Great Britain
by Richard Clay Ltd, Bungay, Suffolk

0 416 53730 8

1

The original Duck Street school was built in 1875. Sandwiched between a glue factory and a bag warehouse, it was a gloomy red-brick building on the edge of Liverpool's dockland. High, spiked iron railings surrounded it and separated the boys' part from the girls'.

Fading photographs of those times show crop-haired boys with high white collars and girls wearing white pinafores, gazing stonily at the camera.

The male teachers, almost always sitting or standing with arms folded, would not have looked out of place on a Wells Fargo wanted poster.

In the years between the First World War and the Second, there were occasional public demands to have the school pulled down and a new one built in its place. The demands were always defeated by Councillor Nathan Tight and his friends on the grounds of shortage of money and lack of space. Councillor Nathan Tight also owned the bag warehouse and the glue factory.

In a statement to the press given in April 1941, Councillor Tight declared that the school had stood for sixty-six years and he was sure it would stand for many years more.

In May 1941 Herman Goering's Luftwaffe made a liar of him by flattening the school, the bag warehouse, the glue factory and one or two docks.

Councillor Tight left Liverpool rather hurriedly to stay on a farm in Wales.

"The country needs food," he told the press. "I must do my bit." He died suddenly a week later gallantly attempting to milk a bull.

After the war, there was plenty of space to build and on the site of the old Duck Street school rose a magnificent glass and brick building. It covered the glue factory site and most of the bag warehouse.

It was opened with great ceremony by a fat lady in a tight dress, who wished future pupils great success. It was called Saint Balaric's Secondary Modern School. All the local people continued to call it Duck Street school. A tradition they kept up when it was later renamed Saint Balaric's Comprehensive.

Today the building still looks surprisingly modern, though the brickwork is discoloured by age and the salt laden air from the Irish Sea.

On a Monday morning early in December, the staff were sitting gloomily in the teacher's room, clutching cups of coffee or tea before starting the first lesson of the week. The morning itself was depressing, heavy yellowish clouds hung low over the school and outside everywhere was cold and damp. The clouds had a look of permanency and the lights would probably have to be left on all day.

Into the midst of this gloomy atmosphere burst a

little round fat man, a sheaf of papers clipped to a board under his arm. Mr. Belham, the headmaster, had arrived for his morning pep talk.

"Good morning. I trust we are rested after the weekend," Mr. Belham beamed, ignoring the muted moan his appearance had caused. "Do we need the lights?" he asked switching them off. The room was plunged into darkness. A scream and an oath in Welsh rent the air. Mr. Belham turned the lights on again. "It is rather dark," he admitted.

Mr. Thomas, the young Welshman who took maths and sport, had pulled up the leg of his trousers and was rubbing his shin with a handkerchief. Miss Lomax stood over him holding the teapot and looking apologetic.

"What is the matter, Mr. Thomas?" Mr. Belham asked.

"I'm nearly scalded to death," Mr. Thomas snarled.

"That was careless of you, Miss Lomax," Mr. Belham tutted. "Please put that teapot down before we have another accident. There's not much time left before the first lesson, so I'll be brief.

"Don't forget to remind your classes to start bringing in contributions for the Christmas party and inform the seniors that there will be no strippers or go-go dancers." Mr. Belham glanced at his clipboard. "Now, the nativity play." He looked up. "This year, I have decided that 2D will do the nativity play."

All the teachers swivelled to gaze pityingly at Mr. Seymour, who had 2D for most of their lessons and was regarded with the respect circus hands give to the man

5

who puts his head in the lion's mouth twice nightly.

Mr. Seymour gazed calmly at the headmaster. "I hope you know what you're doing."

"Don't worry," Mr. Belham soothed. "You'll have help with the project. There's a young student teacher from the training college in my study. He's been sent here for the rest of the Christmas term to get a little experience. He's taking Drama and English Language. Oddly enough the college headmaster seemed strangely pleased when I told him 2D was doing the nativity play. He claims to know you, Mr. Seymour. He wants you to phone him as soon as possible. I'll take your class until you are ready, but please be as quick as you can. I have a lot to do this morning."

Mr. Seymour got up and ambled leisurely along the corridor to the head's study. He and Mr. Bolsover, the head of the Teachers' Training College, had been friends for a long time but they had never had any direct work contact before. He wondered what it was all about.

When he reached the head's study, the door was ajar. He pushed it and went in. A thin young man, almost as tall as Mr. Thomas, erupted from a chair and rushed over, hand extended.

"You must be Mr. Seymour," he said. "My name is Wordsworth. William Wordsworth. Don't ask, no relation I'm afraid. Did Mr. Belham tell you Mr. Bolsover wants you to phone?"

Mr. Seymour nodded helplessly as the student teacher pumped his hand. "I'll wait for you in the corridor and soak up the atmosphere," Mr. Wordsworth grinned widely when he had finally released Mr. Seymour's hand, then he seemed to vanish from the room.

Mr. Seymour reached for the phone. Mr. Bolsover must have been waiting for the call, for he answered immediately.

"Hello, John. Is Mr. William Wordsworth, esquire in the room with you?" he asked cautiously.

"Not at present," Mr. Seymour reported. "But I've never seen anyone move so fast. He left the room and closed the door after him in a fiftieth of a second. He could re-appear suddenly like the demon king in a pantomime."

"I know, I know," sighed Mr. Bolsover. "I've had complaints from my staff and students about him and his theories on child education. He will inflict them on anyone who stands still for a minute."

"So I got lumbered with him," Mr. Seymour observed.

"Blind chance, John, believe me," Mr. Bolsover pleaded. "I had a delegation to see me last week. I'll call them that out of charity. They were more a lynch mob. They demanded I do something about him. I pulled a few strings to get him out of the way for a week or two, but I didn't know where the powers that be were going to send him. I was surprised when they picked on your school and even more surprised when Mr. Belham said he would put him with you."

"My class are to do the nativity play this year," Mr. Seymour complained. "With 2D and your Mr.

Wordsworth, I'll probably spend Christmas in a padded cell."

"I'll come and visit you," Mr. Bolsover said callously. "Keep in touch."

Mr. Seymour heard him snigger as he rang off. He put the phone down and went into the corridor. Mr. Wordsworth materialised by his side immediately.

"I can't wait to start, just can't wait," he began. "Do you know that our educational system does not tap the potential of the children? It's not only a shame, it's a crime. I have some theories of my own that I would like to try out."

As Mr. Wordsworth talked he walked along waving his arms. People walking with him usually tried to keep up with his rapid strides, but Mr. Seymour kept to his own steady amble and, as a result, Mr. Wordsworth found himself well ahead of Mr. Seymour. He paused and gazed about as though at a loss to explain Mr. Seymour's absence.

When they entered the classroom, Mr. Belham had just finished marking the register.

"They're all here, Mr. Seymour," he reported, gazing at the class in amazement. "All of them."

"It had to happen one day," Mr. Seymour said. "Law of averages."

He strode up to his desk and said, "Good morning, everyone."

"Good morning, sir," roared the class.

Mr. Belham said, "I'll leave you to it," and hurried out.

Mr. Wordsworth was impressed by the way 2D had greeted Mr. Seymour. It seemed to him that there was a wonderful pupil-teacher relationship and he looked at Mr. Seymour with a new respect. Mr. Seymour himself knew the true reason. The class motto was 'Better the devil you know' and when Mr. Belham had been with them they were as uneasy as a pack of animals with a new trainer.

"This," said Mr. Seymour pointing to the young student teacher, "is Mr. Wordsworth."

"Good morning, children," Mr. Wordsworth beamed.

"Good morning, sir," the class shouted happily, sensing a break in the normal routine.

Mr. Wordsworth smiled at them and a small silence followed as the class examined him.

"Oh, their innocence, their untapped intelligence," Mr. Wordsworth breathed.

Mr. Seymour took his elbow and guided him to a chair at the side of the desk. He knew they were as innocent as a three time loser in an American gangster film. As for their untapped intelligence, they could probe a teacher's weakness with a skill that would make a KGB agent green with envy. He also knew it was useless trying to explain this to Mr. Wordsworth. He got on with the business of the day.

"Right," he began. "Subject – the Christmas party."

Class 2D's attention sprang from Mr. Wordsworth to Mr. Seymour.

"You can start bringing your money in this week

and we would be grateful for any tinned fruit etc. that you can spare from home."

He paused and there was a murmur of approval. "Any questions?"

In the front row a hand shot up immediately. It belonged to a bullet headed, red-haired boy, Nathanial Johnstone, known to his friends as Johnno.

"Yes, Johnstone," said Mr. Seymour.

"What," he complained, pointing to Mr. Wordsworth, "is he doing here?" Johnno had given the matter some thought. One teacher he felt, was bad enough. Two were surplus to requirements.

"The headmaster has picked 2D to do a play this year," Mr. Seymour paused and there was a murmur of interest.

"That's nice," Johnno said kindly. "But what's he . . ."

"Mr. Wordsworth is here to assist me, Johnstone," Mr. Seymour interrupted. He looked over at the young teacher who was perched on the edge of his chair almost quivering with eagerness, and decided to throw him in at the deep end. "Mr. Wordsworth will explain it himself."

Mr. Wordsworth leapt from his chair and faced the class with a suddenness that startled them.

"One of my subjects is drama," he began.

"What?" Johnno interrupted.

"Acting," Mr. Wordsworth said, "acting. We are going to do a nativity play."

Mr. Seymour elaborated. "It's the three wise men, our

Lady, Saint Joseph in the stable. You must all know it."

"Of course," Johnno admitted.

Mr. Wordsworth, tired of this interruption, said, "First we'll cast the shepherds."

"I'm not washing any sheep at night time," Johnno said.

Mr. Seymour heaved a sigh. "Nobody's asking you to wash sheep, Johnstone."

"They did in the hymn," Johnno replied.

Mr. Wordsworth looked at Mr. Seymour helplessly. Mr. Seymour answered for him. "They weren't washing them, Johnstone, they were *watching* them."

"What was they doing?" Johnno asked, interested despite himself.

"They wasn't doing . . ." Mr. Seymour paused. "They weren't doing anything."

"Then what were they watching them for?" Johnno persisted, determined to get the root of the matter.

"To stop them getting nicked," Mr. Seymour snarled. "Now shut up."

"I'll pick a girl to be Our Lady," Mr. Wordsworth gazed about the class.

"Please, sir," Nellie Allbright put her hand up. "Bags me be Our Lady."

The class sat in stunned silence. Even Mrs. Allbright would admit that Nellie was homely.

"You don't look like Our Lady," Mr. Wordsworth said kindly, dismissing the matter.

Bartholomew Webster, known to the class as Brain, put his hand up.

"Yes?" Mr. Wordsworth asked.

"No one knows what Our Lady looked like," Brain said. "So how do you know that Nellie doesn't look like her?"

Mr. Wordsworth paused and scratched his head. Mr. Seymour came to his rescue. "What we mean, Nellie, is that you don't look like the image people have of Our Lady."

"That's not my fault," Nellie objected.

"True," said Mr. Seymour. "Life can be cruel at times."

There was a short silence as the class reflected on this observation. It was short because it was interrupted by a noise which closely resembled the sound of a cart-horse walking on cornflakes.

Mr. Seymour looked around, "What's that noise?"

"Big Davo eating sweets," Nellie Allbright said. "He's got a bagful."

"Put them on the desk, Davis," Mr. Seymour directed.

Davis lurched towards the desk, glaring at Nellie Allbright as he passed.

"He's always eating sweets," she said. "He won't have a tooth in his head by the time he leaves school."

"You won't have a tooth in your head after break," Big Davo snarled as he passed her desk on the way back.

"That's enough, Davis," said Mr. Seymour. "You can collect them before you go home."

"There's only one part in the play for a girl, sir,"

Nellie Allbright went on, unimpressed by Big Davo's threat. "It's thingy against us girls."

"Thingy?" Mr. Wordsworth repeated.

"Definitely thingy," Nellie confirmed.

Mr. Seymour looked at Brain. He had used him as an interpreter before.

"Could you define 'thingy' for me, Webster," he asked.

"Discrimination on the grounds of sex, sir," Brain obliged.

"Is that it?" Mr. Seymour asked Nellie Allbright.

"Probably," she admitted, having faith in the Brain. "You can get done for it now."

"The play," Mr. Wordsworth explained, "is traditional."

"We could be shepherds' wives," said Nellie warming to the theme, "and bring them sarnies while they're watching the sheep. Then there's the pub that owned the stable that Our Lord was born in. We could be barmaids. The shepherds probably dropped in for a pint."

"They were watching the sheep," Mr. Wordsworth said.

"They could have worked a welt, hour about," Big Davo offered. "I'd rather be a bouncer in a pub than a shepherd anyway."

The class began to take an interest in the project. The buzz of conversation got considerably louder. Mr. Seymour glanced at Mr. Wordsworth to see how he would handle the situation and saw on his face the look of a man who has seen a vision.

"I've got it, I've got it!" Mr. Wordsworth shouted, clapping his hands with excitement. He began walking rapidly up and down in front of the class. Conversation stopped and heads followed his progress like spectators at a tennis match.

"What," enquired Johnno, the seeker of knowledge, "has he got?"

"I don't know," Mr. Seymour admitted.

Mr. Wordsworth stopped abruptly and stood with his hands on the small of his back and rocked to and fro on his toes.

"It's his back," Johnno announced. "It happens to my grandad sometimes. He swears by oil of wintergreen."

"Thank you, Johnstone," Mr. Seymour said courteously. "I'll remember that."

"That's all right, sir," said Johnno, deeply gratified. "There's something else he uses, but I just can't remember the name."

Mr. Seymour sighed softly and turned his attention to Mr. Wordsworth. "If you could explain?"

The student teacher spun round and shot towards him. "Free expression," he said. "It came to me in a flash. You simply explain each scene to the children, then let them interpret it in their own way. There's no script. It gives a natural spontaneity and the audience see the event through the eyes of children." He turned to the class again.

"Does anyone know what 'Free Expression' means?"

"A belladonna plaster," Johnno shouted, opening his eyes and relaxing.

"You're not even close, Johnstone," Mr. Seymour said.

"Oil of wintergreen and a belladonna plaster," Johnno insisted. "I'm right sir, honest."

"Ah," said Mr. Seymour suddenly understanding. "You are, of course, referring to your grandfather's affliction?"

"His back, sir," Johnno answered.

"Of course," said Mr. Seymour. "Thank you."

Johnno nodded happily and slumped in his desk, mentally drained.

"I appear to have missed something," said Mr. Wordsworth, who had been listening to this exchange.

"Very little," Mr. Seymour assured him. He waved his hand at the class. "Do go on."

2

Mr. Seymour was late getting back to the teachers' room at break. Mr. Wordsworth had kept 2D enthralled with his idea of free expression. As soon as the class had realised that they were not to be bound by a script their enthusiasm was instant.

They listened to Mr. Wordsworth, casting wary glances at Mr. Seymour as they did so.

He stood poker-faced and unmoving. They sensed he was not going to interfere.

The bell for break rang but, with the exception of Johnno, the class ignored it.

"That was the bell," he informed Mr. Seymour.

"I heard it Johnstone," Mr. Seymour replied.

"So did I, sir," Johnno said, delighted at the coincidence. "Could you tell everyone?"

"I can deny you nothing, Johnstone," Mr. Seymour murmured. With some difficulty he attracted Mr. Wordsworth's attention. By the time he had prised him from Nellie Allbright and a hard core of women's libbers and reached the staff room they were almost ten minutes late.

"Given you up for lost," Mr. Thomas greeted him.

He handed him a mug of tea. "Should be ready for drinking now."

Mr. Seymour took a welcome gulp and introduced Mr. Wordsworth to the other teachers.

"Mr. Wordsworth is taking 2D for the nativity play," he announced. "He's got some brilliant new ideas and I think he should try them out unhindered by an old timer like me." Mr. Wordsworth took his cue and launched happily into a monologue about free expression and the arts.

The teachers listened to him for much the same reason as 2D. He represented a break in the routine. Someone handed him a cup of coffee and he nodded and took it without pausing. He drank small sips of the coffee without hindering his narrative. He also gestured with the cup, spraying those near to him with coffee. They moved back warily. Mr. Seymour nudged Mr. Thomas. "The lad's full of new ideas. That's why I don't want to get in his way."

"You're just trying to establish an alibi for when the egg hits the fan," Mr. Thomas replied cynically. "You should wash your hands publicly in a bowl of water, then try for the part of Pontius Pilate."

Mr. Seymour smiled into his cup. "What a nasty thing to say, Mr. Thomas. You're very hurtful."

"Cobblers," Mr. Thomas said rudely.

The play and the party were scheduled for the day school broke up. They were to take place in the church hall, which had a large stage and was roomy enough for the party afterwards. Mr. Dickens the woodwork master and Mr. Gamboge the art master became involved in the sets that Mr. Wordsworth demanded. This gave the other teachers a much-needed rest from Mr. Wordsworth, but was rough on Messrs. Dickens and Gamboge who become moody and inclined to snap.

Mr. Seymour watched 2D carefully and, to his surprise, saw no waning of their enthusiasm. He helped Mr. Wordsworth in small matters, such as suggesting that all the girls' names were put in a box with the one picked chosen to play Our Lady.

Though this seemed fair, Mr. Seymour reasoned that the odds on Nellie Allbright getting the part were 17–1. Fortune smiled and Joan Alison, a pretty, dark haired girl, got the part.

Having done this much for Mr. Wordsworth, Mr. Seymour left him to it, refusing invitations to see how he and 2D were doing over the next couple of weeks.

"I want the whole thing to be a surprise," he pleaded, straight-faced.

On the morning of the day the school broke up for the Christmas holidays, Mr. Wordsworth made a brief appearance in the teachers' room.

"I've explained the whole concept to the class and I'm sure they know the limitations of the stage. The costumes, too, are quite good, except for that little idiot Hopkins, who wants to wear a pirate outfit. I've had to point out to him a dozen times that it's Pontius Pilate and not Pontius the Pirate." He paused, a most unusual event.

"Something wrong?" someone asked hopefully.

"No, no," Mr. Wordsworth denied. "It's just that there seems to be a lack of cooperation between the boys and the girls. Nothing serious."

"Never mind," Miss Lomax said. "We're all looking forward to two o'clock. Good luck."

Mr. Wordsworth put his cup down and shook a finger at her. "You shouldn't say 'good luck'. It's a theatrical superstition that it brings bad luck. They say 'Break a leg'." He glanced at his watch. "I really must be off."

"Break a leg," everybody shouted as he left the room.

"Break both legs," Mr. Dickens growled.

Mr. Gamboge raised his cup. "I'll drink to that."

It wasn't until they heard the audience coming into the hall that the cast began to feel twinges of stage fright. The girls gathered in groups asking each other if they looked all right. The boys wandered around with assumed nonchalance, occasionally stumbling over the old curtains and table-cloths that made up their costumes. Mr. Wordsworth blurred around giving last minute instructions, arms flailing. His rapidity of movement had led to him being called 'Willie the Whippet' by the class.

The Brain, who was playing Saint Joseph, stood on his own. He had not shared the rest of 2D's optimism about the play from the start and was the only one in the class who hadn't tried to pad out his part. He intended to go on, say his lines and get off again.

Mr. Wordsworth strode up. "Have you seen Johnstone?" he asked.

"No, sir," the Brain looked around. He had been so uninterested that he hadn't noticed his henchman's absence.

"See if he's still in the dressing room, will you." Mr. Wordsworth darted off. As Brain made his way into the short corridor that led to the dressing rooms Joan Alison came over to him.

"Where are you going?" she asked. "It'll start soon and we're on first."

"Johnno's missing," Brain explained. "The Whippet wants me to find him."

"I'll come with you," Joan said.

As they went into the corridor, they saw Johnno by the partly open fire doors at the far end. He turned his head at the sound of their footsteps and gestured them over.

"What's that balloon head up to?" muttered Brain.

Johnno was clearly excited about something. "I've had a smashing idea about the play. It came to me all of a sudden."

Brain's feeling of gloom deepened.

"How would you like to go on stage on a real donkey?" Johnno went on.

Joan Alison's eyes widened. "Where will you get it from?"

"Old Duffy," Johnno announced proudly. Joan and the Brain looked at each other. Mr. Duffy, who sold vegetables from his cart, was not exactly known for his saintly generous nature.

"He'll never lend it," Brain said scornfully.

"We won't ask," Johnno turned and peered through the slightly open doors. "Our kid and his mate are going to borrow it."

Brain shook his head. "I don't believe it!"

"Look," said Johnno. "It's in a side street by the pub. The pub doesn't shut till three and it's a quarter past or more before they get them out. The play starts at two. It'll be over before three, plenty of time to get the donkey back." He looked at Brain proudly. "Let's see you pick holes in that plan."

"Johnno mate," Brain sighed. "Old Duffy won't have to come out before three. There'll be plenty of fellers going in between two and three. They'll notice the donkey's missing and when they see it's not inside having a pint, they'll want to know if it's gone to the grotto in Lewis's."

Johnno looked uneasy. "I never thought of that."

There was a knock at the doors. Johnno pushed them open. Johnno's brother, a scaled up version of Johnno, stood there, holding the reins of a well-fed but unkempt donkey.

"We got it!" he announced proudly. His mate was feeding it vegetables from a brown paper bag. He handed Johnno the reins and the brown paper bag.

"Keep feeding it," he advised "It'll keep it quiet."

Joan Alison had a thought. "I hope it doesn't do its business on the stage."

"It's just been," Johnno's brother said, pointing to a steaming heap in the playground. "That should hold it for a while. See you after." Then the two vanished.

Johnno handed the reins to the Brain. "Bring it in

while I close the doors." He handed the brown paper bag to Joan.

While Johnno struggled unsuccessfully with the doors, Brain and Joan examined the donkey.

"I'm not riding it," Joan announced, when Johnno had given up his struggle with the doors and joined them. "It looks like it might have fleas."

"Donkey fleas," said Johnno knowledgeably. "They don't bite people."

"They're not going to get the chance," Joan said firmly.

"You'll have to ride it, Brain," Johnno said.

"It wouldn't look good, Saint Joseph riding and Our Lady walking," Brain explained.

"Well," Johnno was indignant, "after all the trouble I went to."

Brain sighed. Johnno was his mate. "O.K. I'll ride it."

"You'll look good," Johnno promised.

The donkey stirred restlessly and Joan fed it a piece of carrot.

"It's got beautiful eyes," she said.

"Its owner hasn't," Brain said gloomily. "He's got eyes like blood-shot grapes."

"Cheer up," Johnno pleaded. "Even if he does get told it's missing, he still has to find it."

"There's a big clue steaming away in the middle of the playground," Brain pointed out.

The donkey started nervously again as a door crashed open and Big Davo staggered into the corridor carrying the smallest boy in the class, Anthony Hopkins, known as the Ant. What the Ant lacked in inches, he made up for in ferocity.

"Let me go, you big gorilla!" the Ant was shouting, his face purple with rage, "and I'll chop you down to my size."

"What has he done?" asked Johnno.

"He's got that blinking pirate costume on under his robes," Big Davo said. "I spotted his wooden leg. He just won't be told. I'm going to lock him in that big wardrobe in the dressing room. He's not going to spoil the play for the rest of us."

Because of the Ant's struggles, he had had to back into the dressing room. Now he noticed the donkey. "Here," he said, "that's old Duffy's donkey. Does he know?"

Brain shook his head sadly.

"You're mad!" Big Davo said, reversing from sight with the struggling Ant. "Raving mad."

Mr. Wordsworth stuck his head into the corridor.

"Ah! there you are. Good heavens, where did you get the donkey?"

"We borrowed it, sir," Johnno said.

"Well done. It will add an air of verisimilitude. Hurry backstage, we'll be starting soon." The head vanished.

"What will the donkey do?" Johnno asked the Brain.

"Make it look real," Brain explained.

"That's what I thought," Johnno said.

3

The audience was in a very good mood. Both pupils and teachers were looking forward to the Christmas holidays. There was also an air of anticipation, unusual before a school play. Mr. Bolsover turned up as the teachers were settling everyone down.

"This is a surprise," Mr. Seymour said, leading him to a row of vacant chairs.

"Wouldn't miss it for anything," Mr. Bolsover assured him.

The noise of chatter and the scraping of chairs died down and the staff, with a last wary glance at their charges, joined them.

The lights dimmed and the curtains opened. There was a distinct hush as everyone examined the scenery. The backdrop showed a desert at night, stars shining with a big star in the middle, out-shining the others.

Joan Alison entered stage left, leading the donkey with the Brain riding. It caught everyone by surprise and applause and delighted 'Ahhs' arose from the audience.

Joan stopped just onstage and milked the impact for all it was worth. When things quietened down, she stepped closer to the footlights and said, "I am Our

Lady," she pointed to the Brain, "and this is Saint Joseph. We have been travelling all day and I have just got off the donkey to stretch my legs. We have to travel to Bethlehem to have our names taken in a census. If we don't the brutal Roman soldiers will throw us in jail."

She drew the back of her hand across her forehead to indicate how tired she was. Brain sat grimly on the donkey staring straight ahead. He resembled a frozen jockey.

"We must continue on our way," Joan said, staggering slightly to drive her fatigue home to the audience.

She tugged the reins to urge the donkey on and as it began to move, a wild figure erupted from the wings and clouted Brain on the side of his head, toppling him from the donkey. Brain hit the floor with a thud that shook the stage. The reins were snatched from Joan's nerveless fingers and the animal and its owner exited, stage left. Mr. Duffy had re-claimed his donkey. Mr. Bolsover nudged Mr. Seymour. "The play is starting off well, I will say that."

Joan helped the dazed Brain to his feet and ad libbed like an old trouper.

"That was a brutal Roman soldier," she declared.

"It certainly wasn't the good humour man," Mr. Thomas sniggered.

"Has the brutal Roman soldier hurt you, Saint Joseph?" Joan asked.

"Yes, he has," Saint Joseph said coldly, rubbing his skull.

Joan propelled him across the stage. "We must

reach Bethlehem by nightfall or face a night in the wilderness."

"My head's spinning," Saint Joseph complained as they exited, stage right.

The curtains closed on the short introductory scene, and a babble of voices and scattered applause broke out. Open hands were swung in arcs as the audience relived again the moment Brain was removed from the donkey. Behind the curtains came the sound of voices and bumping noises. Then they opened again and everything went quiet.

The scenery was basically the same but, in addition, there were three large cut-out hills which gave the impression of rolling countryside. A group of shepherds stood around a camp fire consisting of red paper on top of a bicycle lamp. They stood in a semi-circle facing the audience.

Johnno, obviously the mouthpiece of the outfit, stepped forward. "We are shepherds in the hills above Bethlehem," he declared, "guarding the sheep from harm."

The audience inspected the stage. It appeared to be quite free of sheep.

"What sheep?" a voice enquired.

Johnno glared out at the audience and pointed backstage. "They are asleep in the fold of yonder hill."

"Yonder hill," another shepherd bawled, snatching himself a small speaking part.

"Stop shouting," the voice advised. "You'll wake them up."

A couple of teachers leapt up and restored discipline.

Johnno waited until things had quietened down and pointed to the large star on the backdrop.

"We shepherds have noticed a new star in the sky–," he paused for dramatic effect.

"In the sky," intoned the shepherd who hungered after a speaking part.

Johnno glared at him, "We think it is an omen."

"An omen," the other confirmed.

"Something wonderful will happen in Bethlehem," Johnno went on, ignoring him.

"In Bethlehem," his fellow shepherd was getting the hang of it.

"They must be minding the sheep in echo valley," Mr. Seymour murmured.

Johnno moved downstage. "Yonder lies Bethlehem." He pointed dramatically.

The other shepherd, maddened now by the acting bug, stepped forward. "Nay yonder," he cried, pointing in a different direction.

"I wilt wrap my shepherd's crook around thy neck," Johnno snarled, trying to express his rage and keep in character. He advanced on his rival who backed warily away.

"Good evening, husband," Nellie Allbright emerged from behind one of the cut-out hills. Johnno was startled. This bit had been vetoed by Mr. Wordsworth.

"'Ow do," he said cautiously.

"I have brought thee thy sangwiches," Nellie

handed him a packet. "As have the other wives for their husbands."

More girls emerged and handed sandwiches to the surprised shepherds. Each girl carried a large bundle. Eventually all the girls in 2D were on stage. Both shepherds and audience watched in stunned silence.

"We are away to the river bank now, husband," Nellie said to Johnno. "Fare thee well."

"River bank?" said Johnno. "What are you going to the river bank for?"

Nellie lifted her bundle. "We must do the washing. That star is an omen, a strange omen and we'll probably need clean clothes."

"It's the middle of the flaming night," Johnno hissed.

"It gets crowded later on," Nellie explained. "Come girls, we must away."

The girls trooped off, each flashing a smile over the footlights as they exited. Nellie Allbright had promised them as much stage time as the boys and she was keeping her word. When the stage was empty of girls, Johnno found his mind a complete blank about what came next. He stood staring unhappily at the audience until they became restless. Then inspiration came. He turned to his fellow shepherds.

"Come," he said. "We must see if the sheep are safe."

He led them out of sight behind a cut-out hill and crouched down, his fellow shepherds clustered around him.

"That Nellie Allbright has made me forget what comes next," he complained. "Can any of you lot remember?"

"Something about a king being born and old Herod getting narked about it," one of the shepherds hazarded.

"That's right," Johnno's face lit up. "It's coming back to me now. Let's get back on stage."

He attempted to stand and found somebody was standing on the back of his robe. He was jerked into a crouching position again and his head hit the hill. It toppled over and crashed on to the stage.

The audience jumped in their seats and became attentive again as the shepherds were revealed clustered together as though for a group photograph. Johnno, in front, made a last desperate effort to stand, using all the strength in his legs and his shepherd's crook for leverage and found that whoever had been standing on his robe had got off it. With a startled yell, he catapulted clear of the fallen hill and landed with a crash downstage.

By now the other shepherds had got over their surprise at Johnno's sudden departure and they rushed over to help. One of them went behind Johnno and grasped him around the chest intending to pull him upright, but his weight made Johnno lose his balance and the two of them did a forward roll towards the footlights.

Backstage, Mr. Wordsworth was getting everything organised for the next scene when he heard the hill falling over. Hurrying round to the wings, he peered onstage and saw two of the shepherds apparently doing an acrobatic act. Muttering to himself, he began to close the curtains.

Johnno found himself sitting, legs outstretched, facing the audience. His helper was immediately behind him looking dazed. It looked as though they were sitting on an invisible motor cycle.

Johnno's only ambition was to say his piece and get off stage. He made no attempt to get up. There didn't seem much point.

"All over the land," he bawled, gesturing with one hand and supporting himself with the other, "people are saying . . . argh, me fingers! me fingers!"

The pillion rider on the motor bike had stood on Johnno's hand. At this point, the curtains closed and the audience burst into wild applause.

"Odd thing for people to be saying," Mr. Bolsover mused.

"My Uncle Dai wouldn't let that crowd look after his sheep," Mr. Thomas said to Miss Lomax.

"I wouldn't let them look after a pack of psychotic baboons," countered Miss Lomax, who loved animals.

The curtains were closed for quite some time as a harrassed Mr. Wordsworth supervised scene changes and remonstrated with the actors at the same time.

"Do remember," he pleaded, "this is a nativity play."

The scene shifting was hampered by Johnno and his fellow shepherd who were trying to sort out their onstage differences behind the scenes.

Mr. Wordsworth hurried past. "You two," he

snapped. "Get your armour on. You're Roman soldiers in the next scene." He was beginning to feel that he was in an asylum for deranged adolescents.

The audience amused itself while waiting for the curtains to go up. The good mood that had gripped it from the start was becoming euphoric.

The curtains whirred back and everyone stared at the stage with an intentness that would have done credit to a first night at a top London theatre.

It was a street scene. In the foreground was the manger and further back was the inn. Grey painted squares made it look quite realistic. It was lit from within and light from the glassless window shone on the darkened stage. Suddenly the inn door burst open and Big Davo was revealed clutching the necks of two customers.

"Get out and stay out," he roared, hurling them from the inn and slamming the door again. The two drunks picked themselves up and reeled off-stage with their arms around each other singing 'I'll Take you Home Again, Kathleen'.

Mr. Bolsover nudged Mr. Seymour, "The song is an anachronism."

"Do you know any biblical drinking songs?" Mr. Seymour challenged.

"You've got me," Mr. Bolsover said.

As the drunks exited, Joan Alison and the Brain came on stage.

"Look," Joan cried, pointing dramatically. "An inn. Ask if there is room, Joseph."

As they approached the inn, the door was flung open with a suddenness that made them jump and Big Davo appeared.

"Landlord," said Brain, "have you room at the inn for two weary travellers?"

"Certainly," said Big Davo hospitably, "come in."

Brain looked at him reproachfully. Then Big Davo was elbowed aside and Nellie Allbright appeared in the doorway, arms folded.

"My husband is mistook," she said. "There was room but a couple of travellers came in not long ago. My husband knew nothing of this, because he was down in the cellar changing a barrel."

Big Davo was staring at her open-mouthed. As far as he knew, he didn't have a wife in the play. Nellie advanced towards the footlights.

"I am the twin sister of the shepherd's wife who brought him sangwiches," she explained. Having cleared matters up and beaten a possible bigamy charge, Nellie returned to the small group by the inn door.

"You can lodge in the stables," she said. "You'll be snug and warm, what with the ox and ass. This way."

Joan and Brain followed her into the stable. Nellie left them and went back to the inn, elbowing Big Davo out of the way again.

"I must get them food, husband," she said. She emerged moments later with a cloth-covered bowl and hurried to the stable.

Big Davo stood in the doorway of the inn, rubbing his ribs where Nellie's elbow had bruised them and staring warily at the stable. He had an uneasy feeling Nellie Allbright hadn't finished yet. His premonition was confirmed when Nellie shot out of the stable, shouting: "Women of the village, a child is to be born."

The girls of 2D flocked to her call and followed her into the stable. It moved slightly under the press of bodies and the audience watched it intently. They were delighted to see the Brain ejected with considerable force.

"This is women's work," Nellie confided to them from the stable door.

The Brain wandered over to Big Davo who shook his head in despair. "I know we are supposed to make it up as we go along," he said, "but this is going too far."

The stable lurched and moved some more. Offstage, waiting for their cue, the three wise men watched it move slowly out of their line of vision. Behind them, Mr. Wordsworth was hissing instructions and advice at the Roman soldiers. One of them was suffering badly from stage fright and asked to be excused.

Mr. Wordsworth rolled his eyes in exasperation and snapped, "Get on with it and hurry up."

The three wise men, thinking he was addressing them, strode on stage.

The audience's eyes left the perambulating stable and fastened on the newcomers. The three wise men advanced on Big Davo and the Brain.

"We are the three wise men," the spokesman announced. "We bring gifts of gold, frankincense and stuff for the king who . . ."

"You'll have to hang on," Big Davo interrupted. "He hasn't been born yet."

"Oh," said the spokesman thoughtfully. The audience dismissed the three wise men and returned their attention to the stable. They were rewarded by Nellie Allbright and the girls emerging.

"Spread the word," Nellie instructed them. "A child is born."

The girls darted about the stage screaming with delight, before they exited in twos and threes. While this was going on, Nellie stood centre stage, hands clasped on her chest with what she imagined was a look of ecstasy on her face. She resembled a Joan of Arc waiting for the soldiers to collect the firewood.

The three wise men squared their shoulders and headed for the stable.

Nellie turned, "Who art thou?" she enquired, moving into their path.

The first wise man didn't like Nellie. "What hast it got to do with thou who we art?" he snapped.

"We are the three wise men," the second was placating.

"The stable is over yonder," Nellie pointed.

"We know where the stable is," the third one said coldly. "Kindly get out of our way."

As they passed her on their way to the stable, Nellie faced the audience again. "I must go now to spread the good news." Then she exited stage right.

With the three wise men in the stable and Nellie Allbright absent, Big Davo and Brain became conscious of the audience staring at them expectantly and it was extremely unnerving. The Brain had just decided to join the three wise men in the stable, when there was the thud of heavy footsteps and Nellie ran onstage again and gave a piercing shriek.

The three wise men shot out of the stable.

"What the hell was that?" one enquired.

"I have terrible news," Nellie shouted and was immediately surrounded by the girls who flooded onstage from everywhere.

"King Herod," Nellie went on, "has ordered his soldiers to kill all the first-born."

The girls began to moan and scream and generally over-act like mad.

When the impact of the news had faded one of the original shepherds ran onstage, "I have grave news," he shouted.

"We know," said the Brain, "Nellie Allbright told us."

"She'd got no right," snapped the messenger indignantly. He made an unsuccessful attempt to push through the girls surrounding Nellie, then gave up.

"That was the only line I had," he complained bitterly.

"Rough," Big Davo said sympathetically.

"Hark," Nellie shouted, putting her hand to her ear, "I hear the tramp of feet. The soldiers are coming."

The audience strained their ears vainly. There was a complete absence of feet tramping. Nellie pushed through to Brain. "You must flee this place," she shouted. "Go far away."

"That's the best advice I've had all day," Brain said to Big Davo.

Nellie Allbright gave another scream and pointed. A platoon of soldiers shuffled onstage. Their leader halted them and strode forward. "We have come to kill all the first-born," he announced.

Nellie barred his way. "Thou shalt not," she shouted.

The leader drew his wooden sword and poked Nellie experimentally in the stomach. Nellie knocked the sword from his hand and grabbed him by the throat. A girl who tried to assist her was pulled to the floor by another Roman soldier. The rest of the girls hurled themselves into battle. One was hit on the head with a sword and her assailant was promptly punched by her brother, another member of the platoon. Scattered fights broke out in the ranks and the disappointed messenger was an early casualty. Then Big Davo hurled himself into the fray, closely followed by the three wise men and Saint Joseph.

Mr. Seymour was fascinated by the unfortunate who Nellie had by the throat.

"That lad," he said to Mr. Bolsover, "is either the finest actor since Lord Olivier, or she really is choking the life out of him."

Mr. Bolsover examined the combatants. "He is going an odd shade of purple," he admitted.

Backstage, Mr. Wordsworth muttered to himself and tried to wind down the curtains, but the mechanism had stuck. He was pulling at the handle, his face contorted with effort and annoyance, when the small

Roman soldier who had asked to be excused appeared.

"I'm back sir," he informed him. "Where is everybody?"

Mr. Wordsworth released the handle and turned to his questioner. "They are on stage," he said in a voice that shook with the effort of keeping calm. "Re-enacting the second battle of bull run."

The small Roman soldier peered on stage. "They're fighting too, sir. Will I tell them to stop?"

"If you think it will do any good," Mr. Wordsworth said.

The small Roman soldier marched importantly on stage, faced the struggling mass and shouted "Stop!"

He was punched in the face and vanished from sight. With a scream of rage, Mr. Wordsworth ran on stage. He tripped over a pair of struggling bodies and vanished over the edge of the stage. His sudden appearance and disappearance, plus the thud as he landed at the feet of those in the front row, froze everyone.

Then Mr. Wordsworth moaned softly and the spell was broken. Mr. Seymour jumped up. "Remain in your seats," he shouted.

Mr. Belham ran to phone an ambulance while other teachers moved up and down restoring order and a couple comforted Mr. Wordsworth. The ambulance arrived in a surprisingly short time and the unfortunate Mr. Wordsworth was placed on a stretcher and carried out.

"I'll go with him," Mr. Belham said. "Take over will you, Mr. Seymour?" Then he hurried out.

Mr. Seymour considered the situation. "Miss Lomax," he said, "There are drinks ready on a trolley in the kitchen. Bring them in here with some paper cups. It will give everyone something to do until the kitchen staff are ready with the dinner." When she hurried off he turned to Mr. Thomas. "I think we'll have 2D off the stage before they decide that the armistice is over."

Mr. Thomas addressed 2D, who were still peering uncertainly over the edge of the stage.

"Right, ladies and gentlemen. The play is over. Come on down and we'll fix you up with a drink."

"He's not dead is he, sir?" Nellie Allbright asked.

"No," said Mr. Thomas surprised. "He's not dead."

"Then you don't have to stop the play," Nellie said triumphantly. "You only do that when someone is dead."

"Miss Allbright," Mr. Thomas said, raising his voice, "if you and your strolling players are not down here in two minutes, the stage will be littered with corpses and yours will number amongst them."

Nellie's shoulders slumped and they trooped down the side steps into the hall.

Mr. Seymour addressed the audience. "I think I can say that 2D entertained us, so let us show them our appreciation."

The applause and cheers were thunderous and genuine. The players gave embarrassed little bows and even Nellie was mollified.

Miss Lomax trundled the trolley in to more cheers and the other teachers began handing out paper cups. Then over all the noise, came a high-pitched squeal of agony. Everything went quiet and heads turned trying to locate its source.

"Yo ho ho and a bottle of rum," shouted a voice onstage, and Anthony Hopkins, the Ant, was seen to be clinging to the curtains, stage left. The Ant had finally broken out of the wardrobe and had headed for the stage in a vile temper. He had lost his crutch in the struggle with Big Davo and had discovered that his wooden leg was rather short. On top of this, his real leg had been bent back and tied to a scout belt for some considerable time and now it was developing a painful cramp.

"Avast and belay," he shouted, leaving the safety of the curtain and advancing across the stage. He had everyone's attention. They watched his progress with fascination. Shoulders hunched in anticipation of the stab of pain, he dipped down on the wooden leg, gave a squeal of agony, came up again on his good leg, then dipped down again.

"Who is it?" Mr. Bolsover whispered as the Ant dipped and squealed his way centre stage.

"I think it's the Hunchback of Notre Dame's eldest lad," Mr. Seymour replied.

The Ant gave a final squeal and faced the audience.

"I am the captain of a pirate ship that has just docked in Bethlehem," he shouted. "I am feared all over the world."

"Especially by pirate ship owners," Mr. Seymour murmured. "Bethlehem is thirty five miles inland."

"My name," the Ant shouted dramatically – he paused and drew his cutlass, leaning slightly on his wooden leg. Pain shot through him as the big muscles at the back of his thigh knotted with cramp. The Ant dropped his cutlass and clawed at the buckle of his scout's belt to release his leg, giving yelps of pain all the time. When he finally succeeded, his baggy pirate trousers fell down.

The audience burst into wild applause. His leg was so numb it could not support him and with an agonised scream, he sank to the floor.

"He might be a lousy navigator," Mr. Bolsover said, "But he certainly knows how to grip an audience."

There wasn't much applause, the audience was laughing too much.

Mr. Seymour headed towards the stage.

The Christmas party was voted a complete success. And 2D were congratulated time and again on the play. Eventually everyone left after wishing the teachers the compliments of the season and all the best.

Later the teachers sprawled comfortably in the teachers' room sharing a Christmas drink and the pleasant anticipation of the holidays. This year they stayed back a little longer than usual waiting for Mr. Belham and his report on Mr. Wordsworth's condition.

When the headmaster finally arrived, he looked surprised and indignant at the roar of laughter that went up when he announced, "He's broken a leg."

4

Mr. Thomas parked his car, locked it and limped towards the school. He had played in a match on Saturday that was widely advertised as a friendly. As things turned out, the promoters could have been prosecuted under the Trades Description Act. In addition to the limp, he had a magnificent black eye and a piece of sticking plaster across the bridge of his nose.

As it was early, he was surprised to see Johnno and Brain bearing down on him. They seemed in high good humour.

"Good morning, sir," they chorused, examining him closely.

"Can I carry your case, sir?" Johnno asked.

Mr. Thomas looked at him warily with his good eye and handed over his briefcase.

"You'll be able to limp better without the case," Johnno assured him.

"I thought I was limping rather well with it," Mr. Thomas grunted.

As they made their way towards the main doors of the school, they passed a small group of sixth formers who also examined Mr. Thomas closely as they bade him good morning.

Mr. Thomas was conscious of their scrutiny. "Tell me, Webster," he said to Brain. "Do I look that bad?"

"You look like you've been taking ugly tablets, sir," Brain assured him.

"Thank you for your frankness, Webster," Mr. Thomas said coldly. "The condition is temporary. In a week or so I shall be my handsome self again."

"That's good, sir," Johnno beamed.

"You two seem to be in an unusually good mood this morning," Mr. Thomas observed.

"Yes, sir," Johnno agreed as they reached the doors of the school. "Can you manage now?"

"I think so," Mr. Thomas said, taking his briefcase off Johnno. "Thank you for your assistance."

He watched them run off to join the sixth formers. With many a backward glance in his direction, the group moved out of sight.

Mr. Thomas limped into the school and met Mr. Seymour in the corridor. Mr. Seymour could not suppress a smile when he saw Mr. Thomas' condition.

"Go on," Mr. Thomas urged. "Say something funny!"

"I wouldn't dream of it," Mr. Seymour tried to look solemn.

"I must look worse than I feel," Mr. Thomas paused to look at his reflection in the windows of the corridor. "Webster and Johnstone were fussing around me when I came in. I must be bad if I aroused their compassion."

"If I told you the reason for their interest," Mr. Seymour said, "it would destroy your faith in human nature!"

Mr. Thomas fixed Mr. Seymour with his good eye. "After that game on Saturday, I have no faith left in human nature! So tell me."

"Well," Mr. Seymour began, "you know Charles Gladwyn of the sixth form?"

"The bookie's lad," Mr. Thomas nodded. "I know him."

"It seems he's a chip off the old block," Mr. Seymour went on. "Whenever you have a rugby match, he runs a book."

"On the results of the game?" Mr. Thomas asked.

Mr. Seymour shook his head. "On the extent of your injuries. He studies form of course and he must have expected Saturday's game to be a quiet one."

"So did I!" Mr. Thomas said sadly.

"Well, anyway," Mr. Seymour went on, "rumour has it he was offering five to one on you getting a black eye, eight to one a damaged nose and so on. I don't know what he was offering for a limp but I have a feeling that Webster and Johnstone may have a treble up!"

"The little barbarians! I wonder what the odds are on me getting trampled to death in my next game?" Mr. Thomas asked.

"They'll have dropped dramatically after this last one," Mr. Seymour predicted.

When they reached the staff room, Mr. Thomas

braced himself and said gloomily, "Now for all the witticisms!"

Mr. Seymour opened the staff room door and let Mr. Thomas limp in ahead of him.

Inside the teachers were staring at Mr. Belham, who stood beside the local policeman, Constable Dukinfield. The headmaster turned as they entered and said cheerfully, "Ah, now we are all here." Then he saw Mr. Thomas' condition and dismissed it with raised eyebrows and a quick, "Good heavens!"

The other teachers, too, showed a flicker of interest. Then the headmaster called for their attention.

"Constable Dukinfield would like you to make something clear to the pupils," he stated. "I'll leave it to you, officer." He bustled from the room.

"A little over a week ago," the policeman began, "an assistant in a grocer's shop found a large spider. He put it in a match box and brought it to us. It turned out to be a poisonous one and when the shop was searched, three more were found. He was highly praised for his initiative. The following day we put up some posters from the Ministry of Agriculture urging people to be on the look out for that potato bug, the Colorado beetle, and that did it."

"Did what?" Mr. Seymour asked.

"Started a rumour among the kids that we were in the beetle buying business," Constable Dukinfield said sombrely. "Hordes of demented children with tins or boxes with insects inside, have besieged the station. They walk up to the enquiry desk, open the container and something hairy with dozens of legs jumps out and vanishes. Every insect known to man is wandering around the station. There may even be ones not known to man in there!"

"You want us to instruct our pupils to cease and desist?" Mr. Seymour asked.

"Please," Constable Dukinfield said pathetically. "We're going around all the schools in the area. Tell them it's a serious offence to sell insects to an officer of the law. Tell them anything."

"Leave it to us," Mr. Thomas said.

At this point the assembly bell rang and the staff started to leave.

Mr. Thomas' leg had stiffened up and Miss Lomax had to help him out of his chair. He stood a moment rubbing it. "It'll ease off," he said hopefully.

Mr. Seymour opened the door wider for them. "As long as it doesn't drop off," he said callously. "You're taking my class for P.T. this morning."

"I know," Mr. Thomas groaned. "I hadn't forgotten."

Miss Lomax looked at her watch. "Heavens, I'll have to hurry." Then to Mr. Thomas, "You will be all right?"

"Don't worry," he replied. "I'll take them on a cross country limp."

As they went into the corridor Mr. Belham opened his room door and stepped out. "Ah, Mr. Seymour and Mr. Thomas," he called. "Can you spare a moment?"

When they entered his study, they were surprised to

see Mr. Wordsworth. A quieter, more determined Mr. Wordsworth.

"Back for more punishment?" Mr. Thomas said admiringly. "You're game, I'll say that for you!"

"Accident, simple accident," Mr. Wordsworth snapped, showing a glimpse of his former self.

Mr. Belham riffled though some papers on his desk. "In view of your injuries, Mr. Thomas, Mr. Wordsworth could not have come at a better time."

"With respect headmaster," Mr. Seymour said, "I don't think 2D should be left unattended for long."

"Nor shall they be," Mr. Belham answered, "Mr. Wordsworth can look after them."

"Certainly, headmaster," Mr. Wordsworth said, sweeping from the room.

Mr. Belham turned his attention again to the papers on his desk. "The education people have agreed to let us have the loan of a mini bus. Shared between schools of course. Now here is a list of days we can have it, so as you can see we shall have to re-arrange our class schedules."

The three teachers began to discuss the matter.

2D were quick to take advantage of Mr. Seymour's absence. A look-out was posted at the classroom door and they gathered in small groups chatting and arguing. Big Davo joined Brain and Johnno. "Has Charlie Gladwyn paid up?" he asked.

"On the spot," Brain nodded. "We've enough for a sea fishing rod we've got our eye on in the second-hand shop."

Johnno took a flat tobacco tin out of his schoolbag. It had small holes punched in the lid.

"I'll probably get a few quid for what's in here," he said tapping the lid with his fingers.

"What's in there?" Big Davo put his hand out for the tin.

"Don't open it," Johnno warned. "Look through the holes in the lid. It's full of little green spiders. My Dad got them for me off the docks. He thinks I want them for school. I'm going to take them down to the police station."

Brain looked at him in surprise. "You don't believe that story going around that the police want to buy them, do you?"

"Yes," Johnno said simply.

"Don't be daft," Brain said.

"He's right, Johnno," Big Davo said. "Didn't you hear about the Ant? He got a cardboard box full of cockroaches from the old railway sidings, and he was going to the police station with them, when he passed a police car with two bobbies in it. The window was down so the Ant hands one of the bobbies the box and asks how much they are worth. When they took the lid off there were cockroaches running all over the place. He said they jumped out of the car and ran at him like two madmen. They chased him for about a mile and he had to run into the ropeworks yards to get away from them."

"That's because they weren't poisonous," Johnno explained.

"They've got to be poisonous. Then they buy them off

you, that's the law. I think these spiders are poisonous."

"Then why aren't you and your Dad dead?" asked Brain.

"Because," Johnno was triumphant, "my Dad found a nest of them and he scooped them up in a tin so they didn't get a chance to bite him. Then he made me promise not to open the box in the house. He said if he came across one spider, he'd keep it and stamp on me."

"All the same," Brain said, "the best plan is to phone the police station first and ask."

"That's a good idea, Johnno" Big Davo agreed.

"O.K.," said Johnno, "we'll phone."

At this point, the look-out shot inside the classroom and everyone got back into their own seats.

"It's the Whippet," he reported.

When Mr. Wordsworth strode into the classroom, everything was in order.

"Good morning, 2D," he said.

"Good morning, sir," everyone shouted.

"It's nice to see you back again, sir," Johnno remarked. "You must have good healing bones."

"Yes, Johnstone," Mr. Wordsworth replied coldly. "Now I'm going to call out the register and I want no talking!"

He opened the register and glanced around the class. In the front row Johnno was trying to have a last look inside the tin before he put it away.

"Give that to me, Johnstone," he called.

Johnno approached his desk and reluctantly handed over the tin.

"What is it?" Mr. Wordsworth asked, taking it off him.

"It's just something I'm taking to the police station tonight," Johnno explained.

"Very commendable," said Mr. Wordsworth. "Are there valuables in it?"

"Don't open it!" Johnno pleaded.

"Why not?" Mr. Wordsworth asked, opening it as he spoke.

"Because all the spiders will get out," Johnno said.

At the word spiders, Mr. Wordsworth gave a convulsive jerk, tipping the tin and its contents over the back of his hands. He gave a gasp of fear and jumped back, dropping the tin. It hit the desk spraying the rest of its inhabitants all over him. He scuttled backwards, brushing himself wildly with his hands. All his life he had been terrified of spiders. He didn't even like looking at them and the idea of touching one brought him out in a cold sweat. He examined his hands with the intentness of a man bitten by a werewolf. There was not a spider to be seen. He could only assume that the little green obscenities had ran up his sleeves. He felt faint and had great difficulty breathing.

Fighting for self control he asked, "Were they poisonous?"

"I was hoping so," Johnno said sadly. "That's why I was taking them to the police station."

Mr. Wordsworth felt a bubble of panic rise within him and as he pulled a handkerchief out of his jacket pocket to mop his brow, two little green spiders came out with it and landed on the desk. His self control snapped and his imagination told him that there were hordes of the loathsome creatures preparing to sink their mandibles into him. His skin crawled.

"The showers," Mr. Wordsworth gasped, "That's it!" And he vanished from the classroom.

The class was left in chaos with Johnno calling over the noise to Big Davo and Brain.

"Help me find my spiders, lads," he pleaded.

Mr. Thomas and Mr. Seymour came into the classroom and paused at the sight of the whole class gathered in a circle around the teacher's desk.

"What is going on?" Mr. Seymour demanded of his class. "Where is Mr. Wordsworth?"

The circle opened to let the teachers through.

"He's gone to take a shower, sir," Johnno said. "He spilt my spiders all over himself."

"Go back to your seats," Mr. Seymour ordered. Then quietly to Mr. Thomas. "Go to the showers and make sure he's all right."

Mr. Thomas limped hurriedly from the room.

Mr. Seymour faced the class, who were sitting very quietly watching him.

"Webster," he said. "Explain what happened as simply as you can."

Brain stood and Mr. Seymour listened to his explanation.

"I see," he murmured thoughtfully when Brain had finished.

"Thank you Webster, sit down!"

"Now listen carefully 2D," Mr. Seymour began. "The police do not buy insects. It's just a silly rumour. I promise you they'll be very annoyed if you try to sell them any. Is that understood?"

The class murmured agreement, then Nellie Allbright put up her hand and asked the question that had been bothering them.

"Sir," she said. "Why did Mr. Wordsworth run out like that?"

Mr. Seymour hesitated before replying. "It's known as a phobia Nellie, a great fear. Everyone is frightened of something, with Mr. Wordsworth it's spiders. There was a chap in the First World War who won the Victoria Cross and a lot of other medals. He was a very brave man, yet he was terrified of cats. He would shake with fright if one came near him. That was his particular fear. Do you understand?"

"I think so, sir," Nellie nodded. "I always get a funny feeling when I see one of those big orange slugs in the garden."

"Well multiply that feeling by a hundred Nellie," Mr. Seymour said, "and you have a phobia. It's as simple as that."

Nellie sat down, and Mr. Seymour let the class talk among themselves for a few minutes before starting the lesson properly.

In the teachers' room afterwards, the other teachers, alerted by rumours, questioned Mr. Seymour and Mr. Thomas as soon as they came in.

Mr. Thomas took it upon himself to explain.

"And when I got to the showers," he concluded. "The poor devil was really shaken. He calmed down a little after a while, but he was still shocked, and Mr. Belham thought it advisable to drive him home."

"That was good of him," Miss Lomax said. "Poor Mr. Wordsworth."

Sympathetically the teachers discussed Mr. Wordsworth's plight.

Then Mr. Thomas sat up in his chair.

"I don't want to alarm you, Mr. Seymour," he said. "But I do believe there is a little green spider crawling up the sleeve of your coat."

Mr. Seymour extended the arm that Mr. Thomas had indicated.

"So there is."

The other teachers gathered around to inspect it.

"I wish I had the nerve," Mr. Seymour mused, "to ask Constable Dukinfield how much he would give me for it."

5

Mr. Seymour glanced at his watch. In a couple of minutes the bell would ring and the lesson would be over.

"Right 2D," he ordered. "Clear your desks and put your books away quietly."

He returned to marking their homework, ignoring the muffled bangs and thumps that indicated that 2D were making an honest effort to be quiet. Then came complete silence and seconds later the bell rang.

Without looking up from his task Mr. Seymour said, "File out quietly, no pushing or shoving."

The silence continued and Mr. Seymour looked up in surprise. 2D were still sitting in their desks and the whole class was staring at him.

"The bell has gone," he pointed out.

"I know, sir," Johnno said. "We heard it."

"Then why," Mr. Seymour asked, "aren't you all struggling in the doorway as though the building were in flames?"

Johnno stood and cleared his throat. "We had a meeting in the playground sir, and we've decided to tell you that we're all revolting."

"I wouldn't say that Johnstone," said Mr. Seymour. "Repellent perhaps, but not revolting."

"Not that kind of revolting, sir," Big Dave protested. "The other kind."

"Like that Taylor feller, sir," Johnno said, sitting down again.

"Wat Tyler he means, sir," Brain explained. "And the class wishes to air a grievance."

Mr. Seymour addressed the class, "Is that correct?"

There was a murmur of agreement. 2D had great faith in Brain's speeches on their behalf.

"Why can't I paddle a canoe, sir," Nellie Allbright shouted.

"I don't know, Nellie," Mr. Seymour confessed. "Some physical disability perhaps?"

"I could get to the top of a mountain as good as any lad," she went on.

"In a canoe?" Mr. Seymour was bewildered.

"Oh no, sir, I'd get out of the canoe first," Nellie admitted.

"The point is, sir," said Brain who realised that the conversation was out of control, "that all the senior classes will go to summer camp in the holidays. They've been told to put their names down now if they want to go, but no one is bothering with us. We're going nowhere."

"I see," Mr. Seymour said thoughtfully. "You realise of course that it's not our fault. The education people have an age limit for the camps."

"It's not fair though, is it, sir?" Nellie asked.

"All the things they'll being doing and us left behind."

2D looked at Mr. Seymour anxiously, waiting for his answer.

"It does seem unfair," said Mr. Seymour, after a pause, "and I will discuss the matter with Mr. Belham and the other teachers. I can't promise anything but if we do come up with any ideas, I'll let you know."

"Smashing, sir!" Nellie shouted, and the rest of the class backed her noisily.

"Right," Mr. Seymour said, "we'll leave it at that. Now if you'll have the kindness to file out in an orderly manner, I'll start the ball rolling."

True to his word, Mr. Seymour broached the subject in the teachers' room.

"I can see their point," he said. "The whole school is talking about summer camp and other holiday schemes and they feel left out."

"There's the matter of expense," Miss Lomax said, thoughtfully. "The older children have been saving for months."

"Any scheme we come up with will have to be reasonably priced," Mr. Seymour agreed.

"Coach trips?" Mr. Thomas suggested. "Perhaps during term. There's a slack period after the summer exams and before the holidays."

"It would be an added attraction if any outing were in term time," Mr. Seymour nodded. "And if the destination were out of the ordinary. There's a staff meeting this Friday. If we can come up with a workable idea by then, we'll put it to Mr. Belham. I'm sure he'll give us all the help he can."

"I've got what might be the germ of an idea," Mr. Thomas spoke up. "I'll have to make a few phone calls before I can say anything more. I'll let you know what I have in mind before the staff meeting."

"We'll leave it at that," Mr. Seymour nodded. "Perhaps the rest of us will come up with some ideas as well."

Having complete faith in Mr. Seymour, 2D made no further mention of the matter. Then, a week or so later, Mr. Seymour stopped the lesson five minutes before the bell rang and the class looked at him in surprise.

"You all remember the matter we discussed a little while ago," he began.

2D immediately paid attention.

"Well, Mr. Thomas came up with an idea and Mr. Belham has given it his approval."

"Go on, sir!" Nellie Allbright urged.

"As you know," Mr. Seymour went on. "Mr. Thomas is from Wales and there is a big farm fair held near his village every year. There'll be show jumping, sheepdog trials, side shows and all sorts of interesting things going on."

"When will it be, sir?" Brain asked.

"A week tomorrow," Mr. Seymour answered.

"In school time?" Johnno breathed.

"Yes," Mr. Seymour admitted. "I take it no one objects to that?"

The class let out a roar.

"Unanimous," the teacher smiled. "You'll be given all the details later. Because of the distance involved the coach will leave early and arrive back rather late. I'm sure you'll have a worthwhile day."

At half past seven on a beautiful summer morning a little over a week later, Mr. Seymour, Mr. Thomas and Miss Lomax stood by the coach waiting for 2D to arrive.

"Poor Mr. Gamboge and Mr. Dickens," Miss Lomax sympathized. "They'll be stuck here taking classes while we will be out in the fresh air enjoying ourselves."

"Into each life a little rain must fall," Mr. Thomas quoted.

"Here they come," Mr. Seymour warned.

Class 2D began to straggle into the school yard in groups, laden with carrier bags and parcels. Mr. Thomas eyed them.

"What are they bringing?"

"Food," Mr. Seymour said.

"We have food in Wales," Mr. Thomas growled.

"This is to enable them to survive the journey," Mr. Seymour explained.

2D halted in front of the teachers.

"We're here, sir," Johnno announced to Mr. Seymour.

"So I see. Call out your name as you board the coach and Mr. Thomas will tick you off the list."

"Do they speak foreign where we're going, sir?" Big Davo asked Mr. Thomas.

"Foreign?" Mr. Thomas gasped.

"I dare say you can speak the lingo sir, good job you're with us." Johnno said kindly.

"What about snakes, sir," Nellie Allbright asked. "Brain said there are poisonous snakes in Wales."

"The adder is shy and inoffensive. It'll slide away if it hears you coming." Mr. Thomas surveyed the upturned faces in front of him. "At least it will if it has any sense."

"But supposing we meet one?" Nellie persisted.

"It'll have to take its chance like the rest of us!" Mr. Thomas said. "Now kindly get on the coach, Nellie, you're holding everyone up."

When the list was complete, he joined Mr. Seymour and Miss Lomax.

"They called my native tongue foreign," he complained.

"It is foreign to them," Miss Lomax soothed.

"The Queen's English is foreign to them!" Mr. Thomas refused to be consoled. He handed Mr. Seymour the list of names.

"All present and correct."

Mr. Seymour glanced at it.

"Good. We'll have a last count of heads then we can be off."

The coach started and 2D cheered. For the first few miles the noise was deafening. Miss Lomax put her hands over her ears.

"They'll settle down soon," Mr. Seymour said. "When we come out of the tunnel into Birkenhead, they'll be gawping at the natives!"

Mr. Seymour's prediction came true and the sound diminished in volume. Later, as the coach went through open countryside, the passing scenery seemed to have an hypnotic effect on 2D and for a while the only sound was the rustling of paper and the steady champing of sandwiches and crisps.

When they turned off the motorway the trance was broken and the murmur of conversation began again. Then the traffic became denser as they met other cars and trucks making for the same destination. The coach slowed to a crawl so 2D began communal singing to pass the time. Being staunch individualists there were as many as three songs being sung at the same time, each group trying to outdo the other in volume.

After a bit the teachers noticed that the driver was becoming a little restless and Mr. Seymour quietened his pupils down and pointed out the advantages of everyone singing the same song.

Class 2D considered the novelty value of the idea. Then Johnno asked, "What'll we sing sir?"

Mr. Thomas suggested 'Ten Green Bottles'.

Big Davo started the singing, but upped the number of bottles to a hundred.

They had seventy three bottles left and the driver's knuckles where showing white on the steering wheel, when they arrived at their destination.

"Can we go around on our own, sir?" Nellie Allbright pleaded, when they had scrambled off the bus.

Mr. Seymour nodded. "Very well, but I want you all back here by the coach at four o'clock."

"We should have told them to keep together," Miss Lomax fretted after they had gone.

"It wasn't necessary," Mr. Seymour assured her. "They are in strange territory. Tribal instinct will keep them together!"

The fair proper was outside the village and 2D homed in on the sound of music coming from the loudspeakers. They passed pens full of cattle and sheep. The animal smells and the noise were strange and exciting to 2D. All sorts of events seemed to be going on at once. In one field, huge shire horses with gleaming coats were being judged and in another, small girls jumped ponies over obstacles. Nellie and the girls watched enviously until the boys became bored and they moved on.

There was a flower show in a large marquee and the girls went in oohing and ahhing at the display, while the lads decided to give it a miss and try their luck on nearby stalls. They threw for coconuts, rolled pennies, fired air rifles and watched young men swinging a huge wooden hammer, trying to ring a bell on the Test Your Strength machine.

After a bit they had spent all their money and were tired of watching others compete. "Someone go and see what's keeping the girls and we'll move on," suggested Brain.

Johnno slipped into the tent to see what was going on.

"They've bought draw tickets and they won't come out until the draw is over," he reported when he came back.

"How long will that be?" Brain asked exasperated.

"Any minute now," Johnno said.

It seemed ages before Nellie and the girls came out of the tent chatting excitedly and bearing between them a large wicker hamper.

"Where did you get the hamper from?" Brain asked.

"I won it!" Nellie said proudly. "It's full of cakes and lemonade and stuff. We can sit here and have a look."

"No. Let's go to the duck pond, Nellie," Johnno said. "Remember we passed it coming here. We could sit and feed the ducks."

"That would be nice," Joan Alison said, looking at Nellie pleadingly.

"Would it," Nellie said with some suspicion. "All right but you lads can carry the hamper."

Big Davo leapt forward and hefted it on to his shoulder and they moved off towards the duck pond.

The field containing the duck pond had no other attractions and was quiet and peaceful. 2D gathered round as Nellie opened the hamper. Its contents bought gasps of delight from everyone. There was even a linen tablecloth to spread on the grass.

The boys stood impatiently as the girls portioned out the food, but waited politely for Nellie to give the word.

"Right," she said eventually. "Get stuck in."

There was no conversation until the sharp edge of their hunger was blunted, then Nellie, waving a fly away from the blackcurrant tart she was holding said, "We took some lovely photos in the flower tent, all of us together."

"Who held the camera?" Brain asked.

Nellie had just bitten her tart in two and was for the moment incapable of conversation.

"Some lady," Joan Alison answered for her. "Nellie asked her if she would."

Nellie dispatched the half of tart. "Have you taken any photos?"

"Not yet," Big Davo admitted.

Nellie popped the remaining half into her mouth. "I think we'll take some more when we're feeding the ducks," she said when she had finished it. "Do you want to come?"

The lads, feeling too full to move, declined. Nellie peered into the hamper. "There's only bits left and what's on the tablecloth. You can have the rest of the lemonade."

She folded the cloth carefully, keeping all the crumbs and pieces in the centre. "We'll take the hamper with us. We won't be long."

The boys watched them trail off the fifty yards or so to the tree lined pond.

The Ant flopped back in the grass and shaded his eyes from the sun. "I wouldn't like to be a duck," he said. "Just swimming around a little pond all day and eating frogs. Fancy swallowing a frog."

"The French eat frogs' legs," Johnno told him. The Ant sat up. "What do they do with the rest of them?"

"I don't know," Johnno admitted. "I never thought about it."

Brain accepted a lemonade bottle from Big Davo

and wiped the neck thoughtfully before taking a swig.

When the girls returned the boys stretched, brushed pieces of grass off their clothes and stood up.

"Don't leave the lemonade bottles lying there," Nellie said. "Some poor animal might tread on them."

"We'll put them in the hamper," Johnno offered.

"No," Nellie stood in front of the girls carrying the hamper. "We'll only have to take them out again. There's bins in the village."

Big Davo shrugged amiably. "O.K." he said, picking up a bottle. "Do you want me to carry the hamper?"

"We can manage," Nellie assured him.

They trailed back to the village and found the coach.

Miss Lomax and Mr. Seymour were standing by it, chatting with the driver.

"Ah, the wanderers return," he said, when he saw them. "And on time too."

"Where did you get the hamper from girls?" Miss Lomax asked.

"I won it miss," Nellie said. "It was full of cakes and lemonade and stuff. If there'd been any left, I'd have given you some."

"Your generosity does you credit, Nellie," said Mr. Seymour. "Put the hamper at the back of the coach where no one will trip over it."

He and Miss Lomax saw them aboard, checking names and faces off a mental list.

"We don't seem to have lost any," he said to Miss Lomax when they were on the bus.

"No," she nodded. "All we have to do now is drag Mr. Thomas away from his friends and we can start back."

"He does know a lot of people," the driver said, shaking his head in admiration.

Mr. Seymour stood on the steps of the coach and gazed around. "I see him," he said triumphantly and, jumping down, plunged into the crowds. The driver got into his cab, started the engine and peered speculatively around for the best way to get out.

Mr. Seymour came back towing a reluctant Mr. Thomas and the coach moved out. After a final wave from the steps of the coach, Mr. Thomas guided the driver off the still crowded road into a twisting, leafy lane.

"We'll take the back lanes until we reach the coast road," he explained. "There's a little town about half an hour's drive away. It won't be crowded and we can have a meal in comfort."

He looked down the coach at 2D. "I'll bet they're hungry."

"I'll bet they're not!" Mr. Seymour said. "Nellie Allbright won a hamper of food and they've emptied it between them."

Miss Lomax cupped a hand to her ear. "I can hear a duck quacking."

"So can I," Mr. Seymour said grimly. Then to the driver, "Stop the coach!"

The driver did so.

Mr. Seymour made for the source of the quacking.

It came from Nellie's hamper. He opened it and took out a half grown duck.

"I don't think it's got a mother, sir," Nellie pleaded.

"That's sad," said Mr. Seymour. He walked to the front of the coach and the driver opened the door for him. He stood on the step and lobbed the duck in the general direction of the duck pond.

6

Under Mr. Thomas' guidance, the coach made steady progress and pulled into a sleepy looking little town. Parking space was plentiful and 2D dismounted with the teachers and gazed about with curiosity.

"You can go off on your own," said Mr. Seymour, "but be back in an hour, no later."

2D moved off, eager to explore. After a brief consultation, Nellie said. "Us girls are going off by ourselves. We want to window shop and take photographs."

"You just want to pose when you get your photos taken," Johnno accused. He put one hand on his hip and the other on his chin and fluttered his eyes at an imaginary camera.

"We'll pose if we want to," Nellie said. "It's a free country."

The girls turned down the first side street to get away from the lads as quickly as possible.

The boys stood undecided which way to go, then one of them spotted an angling shop and they spent the next fifteen minutes pointing out to each other what they would buy if they had the money.

After breaking up a scuffle between two of the class who claimed to have bought the same article first, they moved on. The rest of the road looked uninteresting so they turned down a street that ran off it and straggled along in twos and threes.

Johnno nudged Brain. "Will you take a photo of me?" he pleaded. "Me Mam has an album and she collects them."

"O.K." Brain agreed. "Wait until I see something interesting and I'll take a smasher."

Johnno beamed. Brain had saved up for nearly a year for his camera and his photos of the school sports were pinned up in the school hall.

They emerged into a large, cobbled square and stood for a moment examining it. On the far side was a pub with two coaches outside and in the centre was a statue of a man on horseback, standing in the stirrups.

"I wonder who that is on the hayburner?" Big Davo said.

"Let's take a look," Johnno suggested.

As they moved towards the statue's plinth, Brain had an idea and he took his camera from its case.

At the bottom of the plinth was a brass plaque. Big Davo began to read it aloud. "Erected in memory of Lieutenant Hagburn-Layman who single handed charged twenty boers at the Battle of Bloemfrontiers."

"That wasn't smart," the Ant commented. "What happened?"

Big Davo read the rest of the wording on the plaque. "They shot him."

"That seems reasonable," Johnno said.

Brain glanced around the square. No one seemed to be watching them. He nudged Johnno. "Climb up on the statue, shade your eyes with your hand and look the way he's pointing with the sword, and I'll take your photo."

"Right," Johnno said. He grasped the top of the plinth. "Give me a leg up someone."

Big Davo obliged and once up Johnno found climbing on the horse easy.

He stood behind the rider, one hand on his shoulder, the other shading his eyes, as Brain had instructed. Brain took a couple of snaps of Johnno on the statue, then he moved back. The others, thinking he was going to take some more of Johnno, stood around the statue, shouting remarks about Johnno's personal appearance. Brain snapped them as they laughed and pointed.

Then Johnno, now straddling the statue's shoulders, noticed a bunch of lads from the coaches coming over and he called down to the others.

Everyone went quiet and Johnno climbed down. They watched the strangers come near. Brain put his camera in its case and hid it for safety under the horse's raised hoof. Then he joined the others.

The ring leader of the strangers, a lad as big as Davo, stood in front of him and put his hands on his hips.

"What was he doing on that statue?" he demanded pointing at Johnno.

"He was giving the man a haircut," Big Davo replied, equally truculently. "Why?"

The Ant pushed his way between the two of them and looked up at the big lad.

"Excuse me," he said politely. "Have you ever won any prizes for being ugly?"

The big lad flushed at the laughter and pushed the Ant out of his way. "Hop it, maggot!" he snarled.

The Ant staggered back, recovered and, with a cry of rage, hurled himself at his opponent, grabbing a leg and sinking his teeth in.

The big lad gave a cry of pain, then Big Davo hit him and the battle was begun.

Their numbers were even at first and both sides stood and slugged it out. Then more came from the coaches and the lads of 2D were forced to give ground. Luckily Nellie Allbright's group came into the square. Nellie and the other girls hurried to the rescue. They hit the enemy's flank with surprising ferocity and the lads of 2D, encouraged by the reinforcements, surged forward again.

It was at this point that a police car came into the square. Almost as suddenly as it had begun the fight ended. The parents of the crowd from the coaches began to collect their offspring. Soon 2D stood alone.

A police sergeant got out of the car and paced majestically towards them and 2D bunched together for comfort.

He loomed in front of them. "What pray, do you think you're doing?"

"We were sightseeing," Nellie Allbright volunteered.

The sergeant took in their battered faces.

"Is that right, Boudica?" he said. "Well, if you do any more sightseeing in my nice little town, there'll be trouble."

A movement on the statue caught his eyes. "What is that idiot doing up there?" he asked.

"He's taking our photos," Joan Alison shouted in delight.

The class beamed up at Brain.

"Smile, sarge," Johnno advised the policeman. "He takes a lovely photo."

Instinctively realising that the sergeant would be the focal point of the snap, 2D clustered around him.

"Smile," Brain called.

2D bared their teeth.

Brain snapped them and, to his annoyance, the sergeant realised that he too was smiling at the camera.

"Stop this nonsense!" he snapped, fixing his face into an official scowl. "Get down off that statue."

He pushed through 2D and locked his car door. "I will escort you back to your coach."

"You're very kind," Nellie said courteously. "But you needn't bother."

"I insist," the sergeant said coldly.

With the sergeant herding them, the class straggled back the way they had come. There was little conversation.

Alerted by the smallest girl in the class who had been entrusted with the valuables, the teachers were waiting by the coach. Their eyes went from the battle scarred 2D to the sergeant.

The sergeant spoke first. "Did you ever," he said, "see a cowboy picture where the sheriff orders the baddies to be out of town by sundown?"

The teachers nodded mutely.

"Well," said the sergeant, "I don't want this crowd to wait that long. Do you grasp my meaning?"

"You have made yourself very clear, sergeant," Mr. Seymour said.

"Excellent," the sergeant nodded. He did a smart about turn and strode away.

"Everyone get on the coach," Mr. Seymour ordered. His only wish now was to get everyone back to school without a further disaster.

7

The teachers of Duck Street School were relaxing in their staffroom when there was a heavy, authoritative knock on the door. All conversation ceased immediately, as though it had been switched off.

"Come in," Mr. Seymour called.

Constable Dukinfield appeared in the doorway.

"Good morning," he said cheerfully. "Any chance of a cup of tea?"

"Ah," Mr. Seymour said. "This is not then an official visit?"

"Good heavens, no!" Constable Dukinfield came into the room and removed his helmet. "It's just that a largish hole has appeared on that wasteland immediately opposite the school and I was wondering if you could throw any light on the matter."

"I'm afraid we can't help you," Mr. Thomas said, after glancing at his fellow teachers, who were shaking their heads.

"Pity," the Constable said. "It was an old lady who drew my attention to it. Her pekinese had fallen down it and couldn't get out."

"The poor thing," Miss Lomax breathed.

"Vicious brute!" Constable Dukinfield contradicted. "Bit the back of my boot. Tried for my ankle but couldn't get high enough."

"Still, the old lady was grateful I suppose?" Miss Lomax encouraged.

"She threatened to report me to the Chief Constable," he said sombrely. "She didn't like the way I was holding it. I was only trying to stop the demented creature from sinking its fangs into my wrist."

The teachers were tutt-tutting and shaking their heads in sympathy, when the door opened and Mr. Gamboge bustled in.

"Morning everyone," he called, throwing his briefcase on to his chair and making for the teapot. "An odd thing happened a few moments ago," he said. "I had just finished locking my car when I heard a yell. It came from the front of the school and when I walked round, I found the postman sitting in a shallow hole in front of the main entrance."

"Was he hurt?" Constable Dukinfield asked.

Mr. Gamboge shook his head. "When I arrived he had his mailbag on his lap and he was delivering a monologue on the care, upkeep and training of children. He didn't see me and I left him to it."

He lifted his briefcase off his chair and was about to sit down when the staffroom door crashed open revealing the school caretaker. He was trembling and the knees of his overalls were torn.

"Mr. Croft," said Mr. Seymour. "Whatever happened?"

"I fell down a stinking great hole," the caretaker snarled. "At the back of the boilerhouse."

"There's a lot of it about," Mr. Seymour said.

Mr. Croft saw Constable Dukinfield and advanced on him, one heavily tattooed forearm extended.

"Look at that!" he commanded, thrusting it under the constable's nose.

Constable Dukinfield found himself gazing at a brightly coloured young lady in a grass skirt.

"She's very pretty," he said courteously.

"You should see the one on his chest," Mr. Thomas said. "She's even better!"

"I was not," Mr. Croft said coldly, "referring to my tattoo. I was showing you the lump on my arm where I fell down the hole."

"The postman fell down a hole this morning," Miss Lomax told him.

The caretaker forgot his injuries. "What was the postman doing behind my boilerhouse?"

"He fell down his own hole," Mr. Seymour said.

"That's all right then." Mr. Croft was a fair-minded man. People had a right to fall down their own holes.

"The problem remains," Mr. Seymour said. "Who is digging these holes?"

Mr. Thomas opened his mouth to reply and kept it open as the staffroom door crashed back again and Mr. Belham lurched in supporting a heavily built lady with laddered tights.

"This is Mrs. Mottram of the kitchen staff," he

said, helping her to a seat. "I found her in a distressed condition in the playground."

"Whatever happened?" Miss Lomax asked.

"I slept in this morning," Mrs. Mottram sobbed. "So I took a short cut through a gap in the railing in Duck Street. I hadn't taken two steps before I fell down a great big hole."

She pulled a minute handkerchief from her handbag and blew her nose.

Miss Lomax fluttered around her making sympathetic noises.

Constable Dukinfield stood and replaced his helmet. "I think we all know where these human moles are based," he said. "I will leave the matter in your hands. Good morning." He made a stately exit.

Mr. Belham gazed about in amazement. "What is going on?"

The teachers explained and the headmaster was indignant.

"The culprits must be found," he ordered.

"It shouldn't be too difficult," Mr. Seymour said thoughtfully. "All we have to do is examine everyone's hands. I'll wager our excavators are sporting blisters."

"There'll be muscular stiffness too," Mr. Thomas grinned.

"Excellent," Mr. Belham began. "I want —" He broke off and heads turned as the staffroom door crashed open once more, revealing Constable Dukinfield.

"There's another one behind the dining hall," he reported, brushing soil off his uniform. Then he left, closing the door with rather more force than was necessary.

After calling the register, Mr. Seymour closed the book and began checking hands. Within seconds, he knew he was in blister country and the owners were told to remain seated when the bell rang for break. Then, without explanation he began the lesson. When the bell rang, those who were innocent left the classroom throwing pitying glances at the seated culprits.

When the classroom was empty of all but the guilty, Mr. Seymour had them line up in front of him.

"I want you all to put your hands on your heads, then lean forward slowly and touch your toes," he ordered.

After a moment's hesitation, they obeyed and the air was filled with moans and whimpers. Most gave up and stood with the palms of their hands pressed gently into the small of their backs.

"Like a mass advertisement for back ache," Mr. Seymour remarked with satisfaction. "Now perhaps you will have the kindness to tell me why you are digging holes all over the place."

Johnno shuffled out of the line up, leaning forward and rubbing his back.

"You have some intelligence to convey, Quasimodo?" Mr. Seymour enquired.

"It was a bloke on the telly who gave us the idea, sir," Johnno said. "He was on a kid's programme."

Mr. Seymour shook his head sadly. "Whatever happened to Muffin the Mule? Do go on."

"He had whiskers, sir," the Ant volunteered. "And he knew a lot about bottles and things."

Suddenly there was a babel of voices explaining and Mr. Seymour held up his hands for silence. Then he sought out Brain.

"Webster," he pleaded, "explain the matter in as few words as possible."

"Well, sir," Brain began. "The bloke on the telly made lots of money digging up old bottles and jars on disused rubbish dumps. He cleaned them up and sold them."

"I understand," Mr. Seymour interrupted. "Now explain the holes."

"Yes, sir," said Brain. "Well the next day a couple of us went to the library to change our books and there was an exhibition of the district years ago, postcards and paintings, sir, and there was an old map that showed a tip where the school stands. So we thought we could make some money." He looked at the teacher hopefully. "So they weren't really holes, sir, but archaeological excavations."

"I'm afraid that the four people who fell into your archaeological excavations would regard them as holes," Mr. Seymour said grimly. "Especially Constable Dukinfield."

"What will happen to us, sir?" Big Davo asked plantively.

Mr. Seymour shrugged. "I don't know, that is up to the headmaster." He looked at Nellie Allbright and Joan Alison.

"Were you two ladies wielding shovels?"

"No, sir," Nellie said with quiet dignity, "we had pickaxes."

Mr. Seymour nodded. "Just as a matter of interest, did you find anything?"

"No, sir," Brain said sadly.

"I did, sir," said the Ant. "A rare artifact."

Mr. Seymour looked at him. "An artifact?"

Johnno paused in his efforts to stand up straight. "That's a thing you find when you dig holes sir," he explained.

"Thank you, Johnstone," Mr. Seymour said.

"What was the nature of this artifact?" Mr. Seymour asked.

"A rusty old carburettor, sir," Brain said.

"Carburettors are not rare, Hopkins," Mr. Seymour explained. "Rusty or otherwise."

"This one is early Roman, sir," the Ant said earnestly. "Probably off a chariot."

Mr. Seymour looked at him thoughtfully.

"I wish we could have dug deeper," the Ant added. "I might have found the chariot."

8

The next morning Mr. Seymour brought up the case of the mysterious holes. There was no need to knock on the desk with his ruler to get the class's attention. He had it in full.

"The Headmaster and I have discussed the matter of your excavations, and he has decided that because your motive was curiosity and not hooliganism, to take no further action."

A cheer went up and chattering started. Mr. Seymour held up his hands for silence. "You must also be grateful for the good nature of those who fell in the holes. They, too, are willing to let the matter drop."

He gazed at the faces beaming up at him. "I have two further items of good news to impart. Firstly, Mr. Wordsworth will be joining us for a week or two starting this afternoon."

"Will we be doing another play, sir?" Nellie Allbright asked.

"Not if the staff have any say in the matter," Mr. Seymour assured her.

"How's his leg, sir?" Johnno asked.

"It has healed well," Mr. Seymour replied.

"That's nice," said Johnno.

Mr. Seymour looked more closely at Johnno. "Why are you sitting in that peculiar position, Johnstone?"

"I'm a little stiff, sir," Johnno explained.

"You would be," said Mr. Seymour. "Now before I give you the third bit of good news, I must explain that the headmaster was quite impressed by your out-of-school interest in archaeology. It makes a pleasant change from your usual obsessions so, later this morning, I will be showing the class the correct way to mark out and excavate an archaeological site."

The news was greeted with mixed reactions. The supple members of the class were delighted with the idea. While those whose muscles were stiff and hands blistered were distinctly less keen.

"That's very kind of you, sir," said Brain. "But we've lost interest in that kind of thing."

"I shall revive it, Webster," Mr. Seymour promised.

"My Dad said if I touched his spade again, he would wrap it round my neck," Johnno complained.

"If your father were to write a book on child care, Johnstone," Mr. Seymour said, "I think he would have a best seller on his hands!"

"That's all very well, sir," Nellie Allbright complained, "but you can't dig without tools."

"She's right, sir," Big Davo said happily.

"At this very moment," Mr. Seymour informed them, "the school caretaker, Mr. Croft, is gathering together all the implements you will need. Incidentally, I do not want any member of this class to approach Mr. Croft. Having fallen down one hole and filled in five, he is both bruised and embittered. The sight of your happy faces could very well turn him into a raving psychopath."

"I'll bet we don't find anything as rare as my artifact, sir," the Ant said proudly.

"True," Mr. Seymour admitted, "unless of course we stumble on a hoard of bicycles abandoned by the ninth legion."

During the first lesson before dinner, Mr. Seymour led them round to the side of the school and halted them on a flat patch by the main gate. Two wheelbarrows containing spades and a riddle stood by the railings. Alongside were two planks and two trestles.

"Right," said Mr. Seymour, picking up a spade. "First I'll mark out the area of the dig. It'll have to be reasonably small because we haven't too much time at our disposal and, of course, it has to be filled in again."

He marked out an area about fifteen feet square, then set up the trestles and put the planks on them about two feet apart.

"What's that for, sir?" asked Johnno.

"It takes the weight off the riddle," Mr. Seymour explained. "This is what we'll do. Firstly the area is marked out and dug to a depth of four inches only. The soil is thrown into wheelbarrow number one. It's then tipped by the planks and shovelled into the riddle a couple of spadeful at a time. It is then riddled and the soil that drops out falls into wheelbarrow number two which is placed under the planks. We then investigate any object that remains in the riddle."

He looked at the faces surrounding him. "Is any one with me so far?"

"I think we have grasped the basic concept, sir," Brain assured him.

"I am delighted to hear that, Webster," Mr. Seymour said. "Now, when wheelbarrow number two is full, it will be wheeled to the front of the dig and tipped, ready for filling in when we are finished. Now go to it."

"There's no pickaxe, sir," Nellie Allbright complained. "I want a pickaxe."

"I'll buy you one for your birthday," Big Davo sniggered.

"We are not about to sink a mine shaft, Miss Allbright," Mr. Seymour said. "Try a spade: you may grow to love it!"

After about ten fairly chaotic minutes, Mr. Seymour got 2D working as a team and the heap of riddled soil in front of the dig became a mound. When the class broke off at dinner time, they had excavated the marked out site to a depth of eight inches and there were patches of sand showing.

Before afternoon school started, Mr. Seymour wandered out early with Mr. Thomas, who had a free period. To their surprise, they saw that 2D were busy at work.

"They're keen," Mr. Thomas commented.

"Perhaps they want to find something valuable before I make them fill in," Mr. Seymour suggested.

"We can watch them from here," Mr. Thomas said. "And it's pleasant in the sun."

With a wary glance at 2D, swarming around the dig like ants, Mr. Seymour fell into conversation with Mr. Thomas.

After a while he looked at his watch and said, "I'll just go over and see what they've found, then they can start filling in."

Mr. Thomas was staring in the direction of 2D. "Odd," he said, "half the class seem to be missing."

Mr. Seymour gave a groan and together the two teachers ran towards the dig. When they reached it they found themselves gazing at two separate pits almost four feet deep with a gang in each, digging like mad. Other members of the school were shouting encouragement.

"Get out and stand over there!" Mr. Seymour shouted pointing to the nearest undug patch.

Everyone scrambled in the direction indicated.

"What is the matter with this class?" Mr. Seymour began. "Put a spade in your hands and you become like creatures demented."

He was interrupted by the persistent honking of a car horn.

Turning in exasperation, he saw Mr. Wordsworth waving to him.

"Oh no!" he groaned. "Why me?"

"Fate?" Mr. Thomas suggested.

Mr. Wordsworth leapt out of his car and loped towards them. He had covered half the distance between his car and the dig when Mr. Seymour and Mr. Thomas realised the danger. They both shouted "Stop!" and made halting gestures with their hands.

Mr. Wordsworth mistook them for welcoming waves and increased his speed. He jumped lightly over the heap of soil at the front of the site and promptly vanished down a pit.

Both teachers dived to the rescue, and found him sitting up clutching his shoulder.

"Are you all right?" Mr. Seymour asked.

Mr. Wordsworth smiled bravely. "I think I've broken my collar bone. I hit it on that damn pipe as I fell."

He gestured with his head and winced with pain.

The teachers helped him to his feet, then examined the pipe he had indicated.

It was scabbed with rust, and on it were gash marks where the diggers had caught it with their spades.

"What the devil is it?" Mr. Thomas asked.

Mr. Seymour bent and examined it.

"It's a gas main," he said. "And it's leaking badly!"

Not long after Mr. Wordsworth had been taken off to hospital, Mr. Thomas gazed moodily out at a huddle of gasboard vans.

"What I can't understand," he said. "Is why they dug so deep."

"A challenge," Mr. Seymour explained, pulling on his coat.

"The original diggers were swanking about their ability, and a bet was made on who could dig the fastest. That was why they were out so early."

"Did you hear the rest of the school cheering 2D?" said Mr. Dickens. "Young idiots."

Mr. Belham put his head around the door. "No heating or cooking facilities for two days," he fretted. "It will take that long for the gasboard to replace that old main. It really is too bad. Would the last one to leave please inform Mr. Croft so that he can lock up."

After Mr. Belham had gone, Mr. Gamboge said. "It was a blessing in disguise 2D came across that main. The Inspector said it was badly corroded, and could have proved dangerous."

"True," said Mr. Dickens. Then he paused. "I'm building an extension on my house. A couple of days off will come in handy."

Mr. Gamboge looked at him. "My garden is in a mess after the winter. If the weather stays nice, I'll be able to straighten it out."

Mr. Thomas gave a shout of joy. "I'll be able to go to Cardiff to see the match."

"Gentlemen," Miss Lomax suggested. "Shall we give three muted cheers for 2D?"

9

It was near the end of the summer term that Mr. Seymour announced to 2D that Mr. Belham would be coming in after the lesson to tell them of another outing that had been arranged for the class. A few minutes after the bell rang Mr. Belham bustled into the room, followed by Mr. Thomas and Miss Lomax.

The headmaster nodded at Mr. Seymour and faced the class. "Listen carefully, 2D," Mr. Belham began. "Mr. Thomas has come up with an excellent idea."

He could see 2D were hanging on his every word and he paused impressively. "How," he went on, "would you like to visit an army camp, stay overnight and spend the next day doing tough army training?"

Nellie Allbright stood up. "It sounds interesting, sir," she admitted cautiously. "Could you give us a few more details?"

Mr. Belham looked at her in surprise. "I was addressing the boys, Nellie. I was sure the girls would not be interested."

"Well you were mistook, sir," Nellie said grimly. "We are interested and we want to know the details."

"I'm afraid you cannot go to an army camp, Nellie," said Mr. Belham.

Nellie was indignant. "Then what about us girls, sir?"

"Well, there's a girls' school not far away," Mr. Belham began unwisely.

He was stopped by squeals of horror from the girls. Nellie was speechless and that didn't happen often. Even the boys were muttering sympathetically.

Miss Lomax stepped forward. "If you'll allow me to explain, Mr. Belham."

"Of course, Miss Lomax," the headmaster said with relief. "I'll leave the matter in your hands." He waved Miss Lomax forward and stepped back. Nellie and the girls gazed at her warily. "Now girls," Miss Lomax started, "I have a wonderful surprise for you."

The girls' wariness deepened.

Miss Lomax appeared not to notice. "I'm sure you have all heard of *Cynthia Fortesque of Clocktowers*," she began.

This seeming change of subject threw the girls off balance and there was a surprised little pause.

Miss Lomax waited patiently.

"THE Cynthia Fortesque," Nellie eventually probed. "The one that captured all the Russian spies and stood in for the ballerina when she hurt her leg?"

"That's the one," Miss Lomax nodded.

"We've heard of her, Miss, she's smashing. We've read all her books." Nellie said, and the girls murmured bewildered agreement.

"Well," Miss Lomax smiled. "The headmistress of the school Mr. Belham mentioned writes the Cynthia Fortesque books. Can you tell me her name?"

"Georgina Vandell, miss," the girls shouted.

"It's a pen name of course, not her real name," Miss Lomax went on. "And she changed the name of the school to Clocktowers in her books, but all the buildings are as she describes them."

The girls all started talking excitedly, and Miss Lomax held up her hands for silence.

"You will also visit a destroyer of the type saved from destruction by Cynthia Fortesque in *Saboteurs of the Seas*." She paused and then said. "Now do you want to visit the school?"

"YES!" the girls roared.

The teachers watched 2D leave the classroom talking excitedly and Mr. Belham turned to Miss Lomax. "You really handled that beautifully, Miss Lomax," he said. "If you can spare a minute, I would like to hear more about this Cynthia Fortesque. She seems an extraordinary girl."

10

Early on Thursday, the first day of the summer holidays, Mr. Croft opened the main gates of the school and a coach drove in.

The three teachers were already waiting. Each had one small suitcase. The driver jumped out and opened the luggage compartment for them.

Mr. Thomas was in high spirits. "We'll have a great time," he predicted. "Mr. Dickens and Mr. Gamboge will kick themselves for not wanting to come."

"What excuse did they give?" Miss Lomax asked. "They didn't give any excuse," Mr. Seymour replied. "They just sucked in their breath and backed away."

At this point the first arrivals shambled into the car park and headed for the coach. They carried holdalls and carrier bags. The holdalls contained their necessities for the holiday and the carrier bags held refreshments for the trip.

"We're here, sir," Johnno announced, arriving in front of Mr. Seymour.

"Again!" Mr. Seymour smiled. "I want the girls to put their luggage in first because they will be last off."

"They'll be on the coach first and get the best seats," Johnno said sadly.

"Hard luck!" Nellie told Johnno. She ran for the front of the coach where Miss Lomax and Mr. Thomas checked her on.

The teachers waited for other members of the class to arrive. A huge rucksack made its way towards them and, as it neared, they identified portions of the Ant. He was bent forward at an incredible angle. The rucksack's metal frame protruded a couple of feet over his head and, hanging from it by a piece of string, was a frying pan that struck his head every time he took a step forward. It made a noise like a cracked bell. The teachers watched in silence as he banged his way towards them.

Mr. Seymour stepped out of his way and the Ant bumped into Mr. Thomas's kneecaps.

"I've had a terrible job getting here," the Ant complained, still leaning forward.

"Why are you talking to Mr. Thomas shoes?" Mr. Seymour asked.

"Because if I stand up straight, the weight makes me fall on my back and I can't get up again," the Ant explained. "It happened on my way here. I straightened up to see where I was going and I went over on my back. I was lying there for ages. Two workmen picked me up and pointed me in the right direction."

Mr. Thomas leaned forward and picked up the rucksack and the Ant. Mr. Seymour unstrapped him and placed him on the ground.

"If you don't mind me saying so," Miss Lomax said. "That was a silly place to hang a frying pan."

"That was my sister," the Ant said bitterly. "She took it off the back of my rucksack and tied it to the top as I was going down the street. I couldn't do anything about it." He paused a moment. "I can't understand her. She offered to pack my rucksack for me while I was having a wash, then she pulls a trick like that."

Mr. Seymour picked up the rucksack. "I think we'll have a look inside this, Hopkins." He untied the neck and turned it upside down. Clothes tumbled out followed by a selection of tins of cat food. Mr. Seymour gave the rucksack another shake and two heavy iron sash weights thumped to the ground followed by assorted lumps of scrap iron.

"What use did you visualise for those items?" Mr. Seymour asked.

The Ant gave a scream of rage. "It was her!" She's gone mental. No wonder I couldn't get up when I fell over. She's been acting funny since I put those grasshoppers in her bed."

The coach journey was a lot quieter than on the previous outing as the boys talked about the army camp and the girls about the school, so the teachers were able to relax.

When they reached Mr. Thomas' village the coach stopped and the boys got out. They were introduced to Mr. Thomas' friend Mr. Evans who had organised the whole trip. The three teachers were to spend the holiday time with Mr. Evans. The driver unlocked the luggage compartment and Mr. Seymour and Mr. Thomas unloaded the boys' gear. "You'll be picked up here by a truck," Mr. Evans explained. He glanced at his watch. "In about ten minutes."

"Make sure you have your own bags," Mr. Thomas ordered. "Look inside."

The boys checked their luggage and were beginning to glare at the village children who had started to gather, when an army truck drove up and stopped behind the coach.

The sergeant major jumped out of the cab, shook hands with Mr. Evans, then strode over to the boys. He stood with legs straddled, hands clasped behind his back as he inspected them. 2D bunched together as they examined him.

He had a face that looked as though it was hewn from granite and they were impressed.

The sergeant major completed his examination and sighed softly. "I'll look after them," he said to Mr. Evans. Then to 2D: "In the truck."

Two soldiers jumped out of the back, let the tailboard down and the boys scrambled up. Then the soldiers fastened it up again and climbed in. One of them went to the front of the truck and banged on the cab roof. The other advised the lads to hang on. The engine roared into life and they were away with just a brief glimpse of the girls and teachers waving to them.

After what seemed an age of bouncing up and down, the truck stopped and the boys disembarked. The sergeant major came around to where they had gathered.

"Leave your kit on the truck," he ordered. "They'll put it in your billet."

The truck roared off and 2D stood alone, inspecting their surroundings. All around them were high wooded hills. There was no sign of habitation in any direction.

"Right," the sergeant major said. "My name is Cullet. Sergeant major Cullet." He beamed at them. "But you can call me Sir. I will be looking after you. If you have any questions ask me. I know everything."

Johnno decided to put this statement to the test.

"Sir," he said. "I can't see the camp. Is it camouflaged?"

"No," sergeant major Cullet explained. "The reason you can't see the camp is that it is five miles away, give or take an inch."

Big Davo voiced a growing suspicion. "Is it on the other side of the mountain sir, and are we going to walk there?"

"That is not a mountain. That is a hill. We are going to march there. Otherwise you are correct."

Big Davo and the rest could not help exclaiming loudly.

"Silence!" the sergeant major ordered. "Form a single line in front of me."

2D milled around with the best of intent and eventually finished up in a straggling single file.

"Good job I didn't ask you to form threes," the sergeant major said sourly. "Your tiny minds might have snapped!"

He went along the line asking their names. Then he glanced at the owner's face. Sergeant major Cullet had a photographic memory for faces, names and physical characteristics.

"Right," he said when he had finished. "Don't move. I will personally form you in threes. If you had all signed on for seven years, I would let you attempt it by yourselves in the hope that you might manage it before you were demobbed."

He went among them, giving gentle pushes and pulls. Then he stepped back and surveyed his handiwork. "There," he said happily. "You are not only formed in threes, you are also pointing in the right direction. We are making great progress. Forward march!" he roared.

2D lurched off with him pacing alongside chanting, "Left, left, left, right, left."

After a couple of miles, 2D began to straggle out.

"Close ranks!" sergeant major Cullet screamed. Then he noticed a small figure a hundred yards down the road. It was the Ant.

"Squad halt!" he roared.

Brain, Johnno and Big Davo in the front rank bore the brunt of his voice and halted immediately. The others shunted into them and each other.

"Like a railway siding," the sergeant major muttered. Then, to the Ant, who was trudging nearer. "Are you trying to desert already, Hopkins?"

"It's my legs," the Ant complained. "They're shorter than anyone else's."

The sergeant major examined them. "That is true, Hopkins. I've seen ducks with longer legs than yours. You will just have to move them twice as fast."

"I won't keep in step then," the Ant objected.

"Nobody is in step with anybody," the sergeant major said wearily. "So why should you worry."

Sergeant major Cullet brought them into camp by a little used path and led them to a cluster of brick buildings, radiating from a central block.

"This is what we call a spider," he said. "The building in the middle is the ablutions and is connected to all the other units. They are empty at present, so you have them to yourselves." He pointed to a building. "That is your billet. You will find your gear inside. Sort it out and put it in your bedside lockers. Then have a shower. I'll be back in an hour."

When the sergeant major returned, 2D were feeling fresh again. After an excellent meal they were shown around the camp. Then they were handed over to a young lance corporal who took them around the assault course.

"This is only a beginner's course," he explained. "Not the big one, but it's tough enough. You'll be going over it tomorrow so I'll show you around it." He pointed to a plank suspended on ropes over a wide ditch. "That's where it starts, then you go under the barbed wire on your backs, then up those rope nets."

When they had finished going over the course, it was late afternoon and time for supper. Afterwards the lance corporal took them back to their billets and advised them to turn in early.

"Reveille is at five forty five," he explained. "But as you are guests, you can stay in bed for another hour. That way you have a lie in and don't get in anyone's way."

The next morning after breakfast, to their delight, they were taken in an indoor .22 rifle range and, after an instructor had explained to them the mechanism of a bolt action .22 rifle, they were allowed to use them. After each had fired five shots, the little targets were winched towards the marksman and he was shown where his shots had gone and he was allowed to keep the target. Then their mistakes were pointed out and they tried again.

After shooting practice, the sergeant major fetched them and marched them along a road that skirted a wide lake. On the edge of the lake was a stout-looking mast with wooden steps nailed to it and from the top a rope went over the lake and vanished into the trees on the other side.

To the relief of 2D, they were marched past it and up to a Nissen hut by the side of the road. They were halted and the sergeant major went inside and emerged with a tin ammunition box. He led them to a sanded area parallel to the road. "We are going to practise grenade throwing," he announced, opening the box and picking out a grenade. "These are dummies. They have a yellow band around them that tells you they are dummies. They are the same weight as real grenades, but they have no pin or firing lever."

2D watched with excited fascination.

"We will pretend they have a pin and a firing lever," he went on. "And throw them like this."

He crooked a finger through an imaginary pin and withdrew it. Then he lobbed the grenade at a drum bedded in the ground. It dropped neatly inside. Then he did the same with another, to show it was no fluke.

He moved nearer to the drum and scraped a line in the sand with the heel of his boot.

"You try it from here," he said.

Big Davo went first and hit the drum with one, then went wide with the other.

"Retrieve your grenades after you throw them," the sergeant major ordered. "And don't throw until your mate is back."

Half way through the practice, platoons of soldiers in full battle kit came running down the road. The sergeant major halted the practice and pointed.

"Those are real soldiers on the advanced battle course. Watch them."

The soldiers made for the mast and began to climb it, swarming along the rope across the lake.

"Right, next man," sergeant major Cullet ordered, indicating that they should get on with their practice.

The Ant stepped forward and was handed a grenade. He stood for a moment with a look of grim determination on his face, then he turned about and strode away from them.

Sergeant major Cullet gazed at his retreating back. "Are you stealing that grenade, Hopkins?"

"He likes a run up," Johnno explained.

"A run up?" Sergeant major Cullet was scandalised. "Does he think wars are fought on cricket pitches?"

The Ant turned around and stood a moment. 2D began to move nervously.

"Keep still!" the sergeant major snapped.

"He's the worst thrower in the world," Johnno warned. "He's noted for it."

"We are safe here," sergeant major Cullet was confident.

"The only safe place is standing in that drum," Brain said.

Three huge army trucks loaded with troops moved down the road, behind them was a heavy armoured car.

"Move, Hopkins!" the sergeant major shouted over the roar of the engines. The Ant began to charge towards them, his throwing arm cocked. The eyes of 2D never left it. When he reached the line marked in the sand, he hurled the grenade. It left his hand at an angle of forty five degrees, narrowly missing the sergeant major's head, bounced off the turret of the armoured car and dropped down the open driver's hatch.

The driver heard the bang, felt something drop on to his lap and looked down to see a hand grenade on the floor. His legs made an instinctive, convulsive movement and the armoured car shot forward and rammed the lorry in front. The lorry jolted into the one ahead and both of them skidded into the leading one which ran off the road and hit the mast. The impact sent a shock wave along the rope and some of the soldiers fell off and into the lake. Then the mast creaked and slowly fell. Other soldiers went in clutching the rope. After the shouting and banging and crumping noises, there was a moment of silence as though everyone were holding their breath. The Ant spoke into this vacuum. "Give me the other one: I'll try again."

The sergeant major turned from gazing at the carnage. "Another one!" he spluttered. "Another one!" You hideous little midget. You have wiped out half the British Army with that one and now you want another!"

Everyone clamoured to know what had happened. The driver of the armoured car was standing by his vehicle, surrounded by the crew who had dived out of escape hatches at his warning shouts. Shaking with rage and fright, he held the grenade over his head and demanded to be given the name, rank and number of the man who had been on the other end of it, prior to it arriving in his lap.

Soldiers came running from everywhere. One came trotting down the road by the hut and the sergeant major called to him.

"Sergeant Hardacre, will you come over here please?"

"What the blazes is happening, sir?" Sergeant Hardacre enquired.

"I'll tell you all about it before they hang me," sergeant major Cullet promised. "Meanwhile I want you to take this bunch of assassins out of the camp for two or three hours until tempers have cooled. I'll try and sort that lot out."

He hurried off.

"Get fell in!" Sergeant Hardacre told 2D and he marched them up the road. They were glad to be moving away from the scene of the crime, for experience had shown them that blame was always applied collectively.

Sergeant Hardacre halted them outside a hut and ran in, coming out a few minutes later with a fishing rod case over one shoulder and a bulky fishing bag over the other.

"A good soldier takes advantage of every opportunity," he said. "Follow me at the double."

11

Not far outside the camp, sergeant Hardacre led his troop down into a disused quarry. On the floor of the quarry there was a large, deep looking pond and several smaller ones.

"Quiet now!" the sergeant instructed. "I'm going to set up my gear on the shady side of that big pool and I don't want any banging about on the edge. The other ponds are quite shallow, so you can swim if you like or just explore."

2D fanned out whooping with delight. As the day was hot, they decided on a swim. The water was cold enough to be refreshing and they splashed about from one pond to another across the quarry. Then they tired of this and sat in the sun to dry off. After a time Johnno said, "We've been here ages. I'm hungry."

The rest agreed that they were starving. They went to sound out the sergeant on the question of food.

The sergeant was resting comfortably with his back against a big rock. His eyes were shut and he was puffing contentedly on a pipe.

"How long have we been here, sergeant?" Brain asked. "We're getting very hungry."

The sergeant opened his eyes and looked at his watch. "Not quite two hours. Another hour to go at the very least. But I'll go back and see if I can scrounge you something. Just tell me, how *did* that pile-up happen."

The boys explained with a great flailing of arms. Sergeant Hardacre thought the whole thing hilarious and insisted on having the Ant pointed out. Then he knocked out his pipe and stood up. He pointed to Big Davo. "You look after my fishing gear. There are four perch in the keep net, don't touch them." He turned to Brain and Johnno. "You can come up with me and give me a hand."

A delighted Big Davo was reeling in another fish when they returned. With sergeant Hardacre, Brain and Johnno were three members of the army catering corps from the cook house. They carried metal dixies between them and a two gallon metal vacuum flask. "They wanted to meet you," the sergeant told the Ant. "You're becoming a legend in your own lifetime."

"Bread and scratch, soup and mess tins for the tea," one of the cooks said as they lowered their burdens.

The Ant was introduced to them and the rest of 2D opened the dixies and helped themselves.

They all felt better after some food. Johnno lay back and gazed up at the high face of the quarry.

"Just think," he said to Brain. "People dug this years ago when they didn't have bulldozers and that." A thought struck him. "What did they dig it for?"

Brain plucked a stem of grass and chewed on the end. "They quarried granite, slate, sandstone. Wales has plenty of them. The Romans dug for gold in Wales thousands of years ago."

Johnno sat upright. "You're kidding!"

"No, I'm not," Brain said.

"Sergeant," Johnno called, wanting confirmation, "is there gold in Wales?"

"I've been told there is," sergeant Hardacre nodded.

2D were alert now and listening.

"You mean there might be gold in this quarry," Johnno asked.

"I doubt it," the sergeant grinned, casting his line again.

"Let's look for it," the Ant shouted, starting a stampede. In seconds, only the reclining Brain was left.

"Aren't you interested in striking it rich?" sergeant Hardacre called. Brain got up and joined him. "If there was any gold in this quarry," he said, "it would be a lot bigger and full of people."

The sergeant looked at him with approval. "You're a smart boy." They sat together contentedly, enjoying the sun and watching the float while the rest roamed the quarry.

"Time we were heading back," the sergeant said after a while. "Call them in, son."

As the Brain stood up, there were loud shouts and the distant gold hunters could be seen converging on one part of the quarry.

"They've found something," Brain said.

Sergeant Hardacre began to dismantle his rod. "Whatever it is, it isn't gold," he assured Brain.

There was no need for Brain to call, the gold hunters were returning to them shouting with excitement.

"We've found gold!" Johnno called as they panted up. He offered the sergeant a lump of rock with a glittering streak through it. Sergeant Hardacre glanced at it and said, "Sorry to disappoint you, but that streak is iron pyrites or fools' gold."

The Ant examined the rocks he was carrying. "Are you sure?" he pleaded. "It looks real."

"I'm sure," sergeant Hardacre said. "It's worth nothing. The lads from the camp have brought rocks back many a time."

2D began to mutter in disgust and some of them started to throw theirs into the pool.

Brain took a couple of lumps off Johnno and examined them.

"Are there any small pieces with this stuff in them?"

"Loads," Johnno said. He looked at Brain hopefully. "Have you got an idea?"

Brain looked up from the rocks and nodded.

"Gather round," Johnno called. "My mate's had an idea." He stood beside Brain as they gathered and gazed at him expectantly.

"We can sell lumps of this when we get back," Brain said, holding up a sample.

"You mean we should pretend it's real gold?" Big Davo asked.

Brain shook his head. "We'll call it genuine Welsh Fools' Gold. I'll bet we can sell it for 10p a piece. All we have to do is start a craze. We'll go around swanking about how rare it is. That should do it! Look for small pieces," Brain instructed. "We can charge the same and carry more."

"Hurry it up," sergeant Hardacre ordered. "We'll be going back soon."

He watched them stampede away, then said to Brain. "I've a feeling you're going to be very successful in life, but in the meantime, you can give me a hand to clear the dixies and mess cans."

"Can we use one of the dixies to put the rocks in?" Brain asked.

"O.K." the sergeant said amiably. "I'll even carry it back for you if you promise to give me a job when you're rich!"

"You've got a deal!" Brain grinned. "Can you find us something permanent to put the rocks in when we get back?"

"Sure," sergeant Hardacre nodded. "There's plenty of empty ammo boxes in the stores."

12

Sergeant major Cullet was waiting for them when they arrived at the camp. "As soon as they return that gear to the cookhouse, sergeant Hardacre, march them back to their billet. Then you can fall out." He gazed at 2D. "You lot change into your P.T. kit and wait."

"Don't worry about your genuine fools' gold," sergeant Hardacre said. "I'll take care of it. One big ammo box will take the lot."

They dropped the dixies off at the cookhouse and marched back to their billet.

As 2D began changing, there was a scream of rage from the Ant who was kneeling by his locker. The class gathered around him.

"What's wrong now?" Big Davo asked.

"It's my blinking sister," the Ant wailed.

"She's in your locker?" Johnno gasped.

The Ant glared at him. "No, you dope," he waved a large pair of shorts at him. "She's packed my Dad's shorts instead of mine. He plays football at weekends."

"Put them on," Brain soothed. "They might not be so bad." The Ant pulled them on. The waistband reached his armpits and 2D were convulsed.

At this point they heard the sergeant major calling them outside and they hurriedly changed and ran, followed by the purple-faced, still muttering Ant.

"Get fell in!" the sergeant major bawled.

They lined up in front of him and the Ant strode grimly out of the hut and stood in line. The young corporal with the sergeant major saw him and his eyes widened. "Sir!" he gasped. The sergeant major followed his gaze and he studied the Ant.

"It doesn't matter, corporal," he said finally. "Nothing matters any more."

"Right corporal, give them their instructions and then march them to the start of the course, then wait five minutes. That'll give me time to get into position at the end of the course."

The young corporal turned to 2D. "Take your time going over the course. It's not a race. The last obstacle is the rope swing across the river. Don't be afraid of going in. There's a safety net downstream and there are two men by it to pull anyone out." He paused a moment. "Any questions? Right then, off we go."

As 2D were starting the assault course, sergeant major Cullet was checking that the safety net was in position in the river and his men were ready.

"It'll take them about half an hour to get here," he told them. "So stand easy until you hear me shout."

He left them and went back to the last obstacle. On the other side of the narrow, swift-flowing river was a wooden ramp. The river bank and bed were littered with smooth stones and the edge of the ramp lipped over the river so that anyone falling off would land in fairly deep water and be unharmed. On the sergeant major's side was a wooden landing platform covered in coconut matting. A rope hung in mid river, one end secured to the bough of a huge old tree. Sergeant major Cullet decided that the knot in the rope was too high for 2D, so he picked up a long pole with a curved metal end and hooked it in. He undid the knot and retied it, then swung it towards the ramp, making a couple of adjustments before he was satisfied.

Eventually he spotted a lone figure come out of the trees and lope down the path towards him. It was Big Davo. Giving a warning shout to the men on the nets, he hooked in the rope again and stood waiting. As Big Davo ran up the ramp, the sergeant major swung the rope over to him. Chest heaving with exertion, Big Davo made a wild grab at it and launched himself off the ramp. Unfortunately he did not have the momentum to get to the other side and he swung back and forth until the rope stopped in mid river.

"Well, don't just hang there!" sergeant major Cullet shouted. "Do something!"

The sound of the sergeant major's voice galvanised Big Davo into action and with the strength of desperation, he swarmed up the rope and vanished into the tree.

There was a crashing high in the tree and small twigs and leaves dropped into the river. A pair of feet appeared briefly waved about, then withdrew.

Two more figures came into sight racing for the ramp. It was Brain and Johnno running neck and neck.

Sergeant major Cullet hooked the rope in and swung it over as the pair ran up the ramp. Lost in rivalry, the two of them jumped for it together and, at that moment, Big Davo fell screaming from the tree and vanished into the river. Startled, Brain and Johnno missed the rope and fell in, clutching desperately at each other.

All three were swept down river. Then the bulk of 2D broke cover and running as a pack raced for the ramp.

Sergeant major Cullet had a premonition of disaster as he swung the rope across. The front runners were pushed over the edge of the ramp by the pressure of those behind. The new front row, seeing the danger, turned and clutched those behind them and went into the river in groups. When the rope reached the ramp, there were only three on it and they all grabbed it together. They reached mid river and hung, gazing pathetically at the sergeant major until they lost their grip and were swept away. After all the puffing and panting, yells, screams and recriminations it seemed strangely quiet.

13

The girls of class 2D were enchanted with Clocktowers. They were met by the headmistress, alias the legendary Georgina Vandell and two senior girls who had stayed on to help. The awe-stricken class were shown the clocktower parapet where Cynthia Fortesque had a life or death struggle with a marksman who intended to kill the Ambassador of a certain South American country when he was visiting the school, and the paddock where she landed her private aeroplane. Then, after dropping off their luggage in the actual dormitory where Cynthia Fortesque had planned pranks and eaten midnight feasts, they were taken to the dining room and given an early supper.

"Tomorrow," the headmistress told them, "you'll be making an early start to visit a warship, but before you go to bed, I'll read you a couple of chapters of Cynthia Fortesque's latest adventure. When you leave each of you will get an autographed copy of her latest book."

She waited until the cheers had died down and began reading. The girls listened enthralled.

Next morning, escorted by the two sixth formers, they arrived in Cardiff an hour or so early, so it was decided to do a little window shopping. They were delighted to find an Oxfam shop and went in to look round.

The girls examined dresses and jeans and then Nellie saw a leather briefcase lying in a basket with other odds and ends. It had a key with it and the small brass lock worked perfectly. It had obviously been very expensive, but now it was slightly scuffed though undamaged in any other way. Nellie's experienced eye saw that a little patience, polish and elbow grease would make it like new. She looked at the price tag on the handle – one pound fifty pence.

"All the teachers in our school have briefcases," Nellie pointed out to the other girls. "Except Miss Lomax. She carries her stuff in a string bag. I don't think it's fair. So let's have a whip-round and buy her this." She flourished the briefcase.

"She does do a lot for us," Joan Alison admitted. "I think it's a good idea."

Nellie stepped in with the clincher. "Why should all the men have them and not Miss Lomax?"

The latent women's libbers in 2D were persuaded by this discrimination and the money was quickly collected.

When they left the shop, Nellie was bearing it triumphantly. They re-examined it by light of day.

"It could do with a polish," Joan Alison said.

"We can all have a go at it when we get back," Nellie planned. "My Mam's got bags of polish, I'll bet it looks like new when it's finished."

A lot of the girls had bought comics in the shop.

They were a couple of weeks old, but at a penny each they were a good buy.

"I'll tell you what," Nellie said. "Put your comics in the case and I'll carry them."

They borrowed a pen off one of the sixth formers and the comics were initialled to prevent argument when they were doled out again. Then they did more window shopping until it was time to visit the ship.

The destroyer was berthed, ready to go into dry dock for a minor overhaul. At the bottom of the gangway two young midshipmen waited for the girls. They heard 2D approach and turned to welcome them.

The destroyer was oddly deserted as most of the crew were on shore leave. The girls were taken around the deck and shown the guns, torpedo tubes and other items of interest. As they left the deck and moved down companion ways, 2D became aware that they were being excluded from the conversation which was no longer addressed to them but directly to the sixth formers. At the junction of some interesting passageways both the midshipmen and the sixth formers stopped completely. Class 2D was completely ignored.

Joan Alison sighed and nudged Nellie. "This is boring."

"They've clicked," Nellie replied. She looked at the sixth formers indulgently. "Come on. We'll have a look around on our own."

Following Nellie the girls crept away and began to wander down corridors at random with Nellie leading, clutching her briefcase like a senior civil servant.

After about five minutes, Nellie paused at a junction.

"You know," someone said, "it's funny, but we came down one flight of steps to get inside the ship, but we've climbed up three and we're still inside the ship."

"We're probably in that middle bit that sticks up," Nellie explained.

"We're lost," another voice claimed, drawing a lot of muttered support.

Nellie rounded on the faint hearts. "How can we be lost?" she snapped. "We know where the ship is, we know where the dock is, so don't talk soft!"

"Then tell us where we are now then?" a girl challenged.

"I don't know," Nellie admitted, "but that doesn't mean I'm lost." Tucking the briefcase under her left arm, she strode to the nearest cabin door and knocked.

Almost immediately a voice called, "Come in!"

Nellie gave a brief triumphant glance at 2D then opened the door.

She found herself in a large, well-furnished cabin where, at the far end, a man with lots of gold rings around his sleeves sat behind a desk.

Nellie stepped into the cabin and approached him. 2D followed, some stumbling over the raised threshold of the cabin doorway. Nellie halted at the desk and 2D clustered around her.

"Good morning!" she opened. "Would you have the kindness to tell us where we are exactly?"

The man behind the desk recovered from his surprise. "I can tell you where you are, young lady," he said. "You are in the Captain's cabin of one of Her Majesty's warships and I am the Captain."

The girls oohed and aahed in delight and took a renewed interest in the cabin.

"So you're the one who drives the ship," Joan Alison breathed.

"In a manner of speaking, yes," the Captain admitted. "May I ask what you are doing on my ship?"

"We're sightseers," Nellie said. "Having a look around."

The Captain picked up a letter from his desk.

"I remember now," he said, "I was under the impression I had detailed two of my officers to take you around."

"They're chatting up the girls we were with," Nellie explained. "We didn't like spoiling things."

"Really," the Captain exclaimed, banging his fist on the desk.

"They're two nice girls," Nellie said coldly.

"You misunderstand me," he said. "It was their duty to look after you charming ladies as well."

The girls of 2D beamed and Nellie warmed to him enough to ask a question that had entered her head the moment she had come aboard.

"Do you think they'll ever have warships run by women? I mean women captains and everything?"

She and 2D looked at the Captain anxiously.

"I doubt it," he replied, after a pause, "I really do."

"Well, that's not fair!" Nellie said. "Girls are a match for fellers anytime!"

The Captain, married for twenty seven years, agreed that this was very true, but went on to explain that matters were out of his hands. A knock on the cabin door interrupted him and another, younger officer stepped in and hesitated "I'm sorry, sir," he said, "I didn't know you were in conference!"

"Don't be an idiot!" the Captain sighed. "You're ready to go then?"

The officer waved a briefcase. "Yes, sir."

"Stay away from the bright lights," the Captain ordered, "at least until the contents of that case are in the hands of the Admiralty." He opened a desk drawer and took out some letters. "Post these for me in London."

The officer put his briefcase on the floor by the desk and took the letters off the Captain, who pointed at the girls and said, "On your way would you escort Miss Pankhurst and her disciples back to two young gentlemen in charge of sightseers. Tell them where you found the ladies. That should make their hair stand on end!"

Nellie put down her briefcase and approached the newcomer, hand extended.

"The Captain is mistook," she said. "My name is Allbright. Nellie Allbright."

The officer shook her hand. "Very pleased to meet you, Miss Allbright. A great pleasure. Now if you will follow me, we can leave the Captain to his duties."

Both he and Nellie picked up briefcases and left the cabin, followed by the rest of the girls. He found the midshipmen still chatting to the sixth formers and relayed to them the Captain's message, then he said goodbye to the girls and was gone. 2D finished the rest of the tour with the midshipmen herding them with the intensity of two skilled but nervous sheepdogs.

The headmistress was waiting for them when they returned from their tour. She gave them each an autographed book.

"We'll always read your books, Miss," Nellie said. "Even when we're grown up."

"Thank you," the headmistress smiled. "Now you must go to the dormitory and pack. I've had a phone call from Mr. Evans saying the coach is on its way."

After packing, the girls were saying goodbye to the sixth formers when the coach arrived. Nellie, covered by the other girls, managed to smuggle the briefcase into the luggage compartment without the teachers seeing it. There was no time to take the comics out, but that was a small price to pay to keep the present secret.

"Did you enjoy yourselves?" Miss Lomax asked as they settled down and the coach moved off.

"It was great, Miss," Nellie said, speaking for the other girls. "She gave us all her latest book, autographed too, Miss."

"Will you lend me your copy when you've read it, Nellie?" Miss Lomax asked.

"Certainly, Miss," Nellie said magnanimously.

Mr. Seymour had been gazing out of the window while Miss Lomax chatted to the girls when a thought struck him and he turned to Mr. Thomas.

"I wonder what condition the lads will be in?" he asked.

14

The coach stopped opposite the camp's main gate and the girls crowded to the side of the bus facing the camp, and gazed curiously through the windows. Miss Lomax kept an eye on them while the other teachers got off the coach.

They had only just got out when sergeant major Cullet, alerted by a lookout, marched 2D out of the camp.

"Here we are, sir," he said to Mr. Evans. "All present and correct."

2D broke ranks and some clustered around Mr. Thomas and Mr. Seymour, others waved to the girls.

"I'm sure they'll always remember their visit to the camp, sergeant major," Mr. Evans said.

"I certainly will!" the sergeant major said, darkly. Now if you'll excuse me sir, I must be going."

"Put your gear in the baggage compartment and get on the coach," Mr. Seymour ordered. Then he noticed Big Davo and Brain carrying an ammunition box between them while Johnno trailed behind with their luggage.

"Johnstone," Mr. Seymour said. "What is in that box?"

Johnno turned, "Rocks sir. With genuine gold that's not real, but Brain says they'll buy it anyway. I can't remember the real name, but it fools people and it's from Wales."

"Thank you for clearing the matter up, Johnstone," Mr. Seymour said.

"You're very welcome, sir," Johnno replied equally formally. Then he rambled after the others.

The driver returned and the coach moved off. The coach was soon buzzing with talk as the boys swapped anecdotes with the girls. Then they were at Mr. Evans' village and the three teachers shook hands with him and thanked him for all he had done and made him promise to visit them the next time he was in Liverpool. Then there was a slightly awkward silence and Mr. Evans said, "Goodbye 2D."

"Goodbye, sir," 2D roared and Nellie called for three cheers.

As they approached home Big Davo turned to the Ant.

"As soon as I get home I'm going to see if my rabbits are all right. What are you going to do?" He asked.

"Strangle my sister!" the Ant snarled.

"Us girls," Nellie broke in, "will be reading our Cynthia Fortesque books. I did like that school, but I'll bet in a couple of days they'll have forgotten all about us."

"In a couple of days?" Johnno echoed scornfully. "I'll bet they've forgotten us already."

"Ships that pass in the night," Brain agreed.

As it happened, all three of them were wrong. At that very moment, sergeant Hardacre was helping to check the ammunition stores.

"Grenades, hand," he snapped, opening an ammunition box.

Then his eyes widened in horror as a pile of rocks with flecks of a yellow metal in it were revealed.

At approximately the same time, but one hundred and seventy miles away, a naval officer with the same expression on his face was looking at an Admiral who had just pulled a pile of comics out of his briefcase.

The Admiral put the comics down on the desk and said, "You do of course have a rational explanation?"

The naval officer, who had been shaking his head in disbelief, gasped, "It must have been those girls!"

"What girls?" questioned the Admiral.

"About fifteen of them in the captain's cabin," the officer explained.

"How interesting!" the Admiral purred. "Do go on!"

"One of them had a briefcase," the officer continued. He snapped his fingers, "Oh Lord! What was her name?"

"Olga?" the Admiral suggested helpfully. "Natasha?"

"Oh, what did the Captain call her?" the officer moaned. Then his face brightened, "Emily Pankhurst! That was it."

"How mundane," said the Admiral.

"It wasn't her real name," the officer cautioned.

"It was Nellie Allbright!"

"I think I preferred Emily Pankhurst," reflected the Admiral.

There was no need for Mr. Belham to be in the school yard waiting for the coach, but he knew that he would not enjoy his holidays unless he witnessed the safe return of 2D. He settled himself on a low brick wall to wait for the coach. It was not a coach which drove into the school yard but an army staff car. A sergeant and an officer got out and came towards them.

"Good afternoon," the officer opened. "Do you belong to the school?"

"I'm the headmaster," replied Mr. Belham.

"Excellent!" the officer beamed. "Do these names mean anything to you?" He took a notebook from his pocket, "Webster, Johnstone, Davis, Hopkins?"

"They haven't arrived yet," the headmaster interrupted. "Might I ask why you want to see them?"

The officer hesitated, "I'm afraid they have a box of hand grenades on the coach," he said finally.

The blood drained from Mr. Belham's face.

"Don't be alarmed," the officer said. "They're not fused and are quite harmless, but I would appreciate your discretion. You know how the press blow little incidents up."

He took Mr. Belham's stunned silence for agreement and said, "Good show! We'll wait in the car."

As he walked away another staff car drew in and a naval officer approached them.

"I'm the headmaster," Mr. Belham sighed resignedly. "Can I help you?"

"I believe a Miss Allbright is a pupil at this school," the officer said. "A Miss Nellie Allbright?"

"She'll be here soon," the headmaster nodded. "May I ask . . ."

"Why I want to see her?" the naval officer finished. "I'll be frank. She has in her possession some top secret papers and my briefcase." He smiled at the headmaster. "I'd like them back and with as little fuss as possible."

As the headmaster stared at him numbly, a coach turned into the school yard. The naval officer glanced at it, then looked enquiringly at Mr. Belham, who nodded. He strode purposefully towards it, but was beaten to it by two officers from an army staff car.

You can see more Magnet books
on the following pages.

Microfish

ROBERT LEE

When Rock Salmon is called in to investigate the kidnap of Arthur Codswallop, it's the start of the fishiest case he's ever worked on. He follows the trail to Ironia where he discovers the secret of the sinister silvery Microfish, the Red Whale, and the strange behaviour of Igor Baluga, the plastic sturgeon. But can Rock find the genius behind the frightening master-plan he's swum into before it's too late?

In this hilarious and gripping sequel to Fishy Business, Rock Salmon, private detective, investigates again.

TV's Naughtiest Heroine in Action

Danger – Marmalade at Work

ANDREW DAVIES

'He is a bit short and young. You sure he's over sixteen?'

'You must be joking, cock!' said Marmalade. 'And I'm not a boy either!'

Can the sternest disciplinary system in the world break the spirit of TV's naughtiest heroine . . .? Or will Marmalade be able to *muck about* in the army?

And also

Marmalade Hits the Big Time
Educating Marmalade
Marmalade Atkins' Dreadful Deeds

The Adventures of a Two-Minute Werewolf

GENE DE WEESE

In the two longest minutes of his life so far, Walt Cribbens finds himself changed into a furry, wolf-like version of his former self! Can he really be a *werewolf*?

After a number of hair-raising and fang-growing experiments to find out, Walt and his friend, Cindy Deardorf, discover they can use his new-found talent to solve another, quite different mystery . . .

Janey's Diary

MARY HOOPER

Janey loves James. Often passionately. But he never seems to notice her. Janey has a dreadful brother and a mum who thinks she should wear a vest to the disco. No wonder everything goes wrong. Will Janey ever make an impression on James – and is there life after school, beyond the cosmetics counter?

An achingly funny story of first love and romance.